Dead Stock

A Bert Shambles Mystery

by

Tim Hall

Copyright © 2013 by Tim Hall

For information, email **Cozy Cat Press**, cozycatpress@aol.com or visit our website at: www.cozycatpress.com

COZY CAT
P R E S S

ISBN: 978-1-939816-21-4
Printed in the United States of America

Cover design by Maria Zannini
http://bookcoverdiva.blogspot.com/

1 2 3 4 5 6 7 8 9 10

This book is dedicated to my partners in crime, Mary and George

Special thanks to Karen Lillis, David Masciotra, Bob Mecoy, Ken Wohlrob, Dean Haspiel, Branwynne Kennedy, Jason Behrends, Ben Tanzer, Carolyn Hall, Chris Hall, Frank and Karen Baker, Karen Catching, Patricia Sullivan, Jen Stigi, Jen Devine, and Jen Artale for the tremendous support and kindness over the years. I love you all.

June something

Whoever said that thing about how no man is an island probably doesn't live on one. I mean, as far as I can tell we're nothing but. Sometimes we share our islands with other people and call them something else—family, career, religion, whatever—but at the end of the day we're completely alone. And if you don't believe me then you've probably never killed anyone.

This isn't going to be easy, I can tell. Dr. Kornbluth said it would be hard. He suggested I start a journal to help me get over the guilt and shame I still feel. I don't have a computer and don't like writing long hand, so I got this old typewriter at the thrift shop, then found a few ribbons at a dusty old stationery store down on Route 59. I really like the sound it makes, the loud clacking and the bell at the end of each line. Sometimes when I'm bored I press the release button just to hear it ring.

Dr. K. was my therapist for the anger management course the judge ordered me to take. He taught me about breathing and counting, told me to eat right and get plenty of sleep and exercise. I haven't really gotten the hang of it, but I still have the brochures he gave me. They're filled with a lot of sayings that I'm supposed to think about whenever I feel my anger coming back. Things like *Wait a day, anger away* and *The bridge you burn today might be the road to a better tomorrow.* I think he was probably in AA at some point.

That stuff about bridges is what got me thinking about islands. Pretty much the only way off Long Island is by bridge, and most of them only take you as far as the Bronx or Staten Island. The other way is by tunnel, through Manhattan. They never tell you not to burn your tunnels; I wonder why. Maybe because they're underwater so it would be pretty stupid to try.

Looking over what I've written so far, Dr. K. would tell me to change one thing: I didn't kill anyone, not really. But I might as well have. I put the guy in the hospital for two weeks, and basically ended his chance of becoming a rock star. He was heavy into drugs so he probably wouldn't have made it anyway, but there's no point trying to justify it. I was wrong, and I'm sorry for what I did. It was the only time I've done something like that, and it was in a moment of extreme stress and fear. I thought I was protecting someone I loved and I overreacted. I still have no memory of how the guy wound up at the bottom of the stairs.

Dr. K would also tell me to begin at the beginning, so here goes: my name is Bert Shambles. I just turned 23 years old, and I'm currently serving a three-year suspended sentence for aggravated assault, because of what happened that night down on the Bowery of New York City. I'm now living back in my home town of Mumfrey (rhymes with Humphrey), a small suburban community on the north shore of Long Island, near the border of Nassau and Suffolk counties. I did 400 hours of community service and took Dr. K's anger management course, but this is the hard part. I have to stay employed and not get into trouble for the next three years, and hopefully my record will be cleared. I have no idea what I'm going to do then; in some ways it's even scarier to think about than what I'm going through now. I should have my whole life ahead of me, but that feels like it's finished now. When I get done with my probation I'll be 26, which is definitely old.

Staying employed shouldn't be a problem, at least. I work part-time at Bonnie's Bag, the thrift shop attached to St. Boniface parish. The Padre there, Fr. Peter, is a really nice guy. He testified as a character witness at the trial, and even promised to keep me employed during my probation, which is probably the only reason why I'm not serving time.

The worst part is being stuck on Long Island, which has to be one of the angriest places in the world. Long Island is filled with the meanest, nastiest people you'll ever meet anywhere, except maybe Ohio. How can I expect to "turn down the anger and turn up the peace," as Dr. K. would say, when everyone around me is a raging, foaming maniac? Seriously. Spend a day out here if you don't believe me. Drive around Roosevelt Field at rush hour, or any of the ritzy communities filled with million-dollar homes and penny-ante Napoleons. You'll see more screaming, road-raging, middle-finger-waving monsters than you've probably seen in your entire life. Long Island has more flipping birds than a London gymnastics team. For as long as I can remember I've dreamed about moving far away from here, and now I'm stuck.

Dr. K. would say I'm feeling sorry for myself, and he's right. He would tell me to "think less about sorrow and more about tomorrow," but he doesn't know how hard it is to plan for the future when there's no place to put down the pieces of the past.

Imagine you're me. You meet a cute girl and start talking. Things are going great, then she asks what you do for a living and you say, "I work part-time at a church thrift shop while I finish my probation for aggravated assault." Good times.

Then there's my name. It feels like a curse, like I'll never be able to be anything good or special with a name like Shambles. According to my mom it was originally Chambliss, but changed when my ancestors came over from France in the 1800s. For some reason none of them ever thought to change it back. Maybe it was some kind of weird pride thing, I don't know. I'd ask my dad about it, since it's his name originally, but he left when I was young and nobody has heard from him since. Phone...

Okay, that was the Padre. He wants me to do him a favor and pick up a clothing donation. It's my day off, but I said yes for two reasons: first, I always do whatever he asks, because he's done so much for me, and second, a good clothing donation could mean some extra money for me, once I've gone through it and picked out any vintage stuff. Which reminds me, I've got to do laundry. It's been piling up in the big black garbage bag in the corner and it's starting to smell pretty ripe in this heat. After I drop off the donation at the shop I'll swing by the Slosh 'n Wash and have a few cold ones while I wait for my laundry to be done. More soon.

July whatever

Okay, that wasn't exactly soon. But what happened after my last entry was so messed up that I didn't have time to write until now. I'm going to try getting the whole story out while it's still fresh in my mind. It won't be easy, since I pretty much have to type one-handed for the next few weeks, but I've got nothing better to do. Besides, if any of this comes back to haunt me, then at least I'll have my version of events straight.

See? I still think like a criminal.

First

The Healey place was down in Pondington, the exclusive and wealthy section of Mumfrey that takes up most of the waterfront. It's part of the original gold coast of Long Island, back when the robber barons built huge castles along the north shore. The castles are long gone, but the money never left. Pondington is still home to some of the wealthiest people in the country, except instead of living in castles with moats and drawbridges they live in overpriced McMansions on Castle Lane or Drawbridge Path. I don't know why that is. Maybe it's because so many people have money nowadays that the whole idea of being rich has gotten cheaper. My friend Oscar told me that the area was originally called Pounding Town, because of the tradesmen who worked along the waterfront, blacksmiths and leather-workers and the like. I like to think it was because the girls were easy.

I was picking up a clothing donation from Mrs. Healey, whose husband, Corky Healey, had recently passed away at the tender age of ninety-one. I only knew that because his death had made the local news. Corky had been a somewhat famous golfer years ago, and was still admired by plenty of golf fans—a golfer's golfer, so dedicated and true to his sport that he refused to cash in on his fame. Corky never did endorsement deals, commercials, nothing. That's why he wasn't better known, but it also increased his mystique over the years. One news story called him the Garbo of Golf.

Even though Corky was retired he still played golf every day, usually by himself, and that's what did him in. He had gone to the local country club early that morning to practice, as usual. At some point he must have lost his balance, because he slipped and fell into a ravine and cracked his head. Nobody saw it happen, or anything else unusual, and the police had labeled it an accident.

I was sorry he was dead, of course, but I couldn't help but think how right it seemed that he had died on the course, with his golf shoes on, doing what he loved. He had even fallen into a big hole. Pretty perfect way for a golfer to go if you ask me. I don't know anything about golf but I admire anyone who can make a living just by walking around and swinging a stick. It makes me think that there really is a place for everyone in the world, and gives me hope that it's not too late for me to make something of my life. I have a feeling I'd make an excellent caddy.

You have to be rich to live in Pondington, and rich guys usually have the best clothes. That's the part of my job that I like the most, that I get to pick over the stuff before anyone else. I don't steal it; I wait for Millie to put it on the racks then I buy it for the regular price, then when I get enough pieces I drive into Brooklyn to a hip secondhand shop that sells it for ten or twenty times what I paid, and I get a nice commission.

The Healey place was very cool and modern, in a 1960s kind of way. It was a split-level, low and crouching and built into the landscape. I parked at the top of the semi-circular driveway, then went up the wide flagstone steps and rang the bell. A minute later a guy opened the door. He looked maybe mid-50s, but it was hard to tell because of the preppy clothes he was wearing, the polo shirt and pleated chinos, the conservative haircut that was neatly parted on the side. That whole Biff-from-East-Hampton style that makes guys look weirdly like old men and teenagers at the same time.

The guy didn't look friendly. He was a big man, over six feet, and had an extra thirty or forty pounds on him that looked more like fat than muscle but the guy still looked mean. His face was red.

"What do you want?"

"I'm here for a donation."

"Not interested."

The door slammed in my face.

Well, it was worth a shot. Why be persistent when it's so much easier to quit the first time, I always say. I was back at the Olds when the door jerked open again.

"Come in."

I went back up and in. The guy closed the door behind me.

"I thought you were asking *for* a donation, the way you looked. Wait here."

The guy stalked off down the hallway. *The way you looked*, that was a nice touch. Another product of a fine Long Island upbringing. I took several deep breaths and thought of palm trees and breasts. I was cooler than James Bond in an igloo.

"There you are."

The lady coming down the hallway was making an effort to smile. She extended her hand.

"I'm Dorothy Healey. Thank you for coming so soon."

She had a firm grip for someone her age. In fact, pretty much everything about her was firm. She looked to be late 50s, which was younger than I expected with a husband so old, and she was still a fox. Trim, with bright blue eyes, fine skin that was attractively weathered, and nice white-blonde hair that was styled very naturally down to her shoulders. She wore a strand of pearls and a very simple, white and blue sleeveless dress.

"I'm sorry for the confusion. Bill didn't realize that I had called Father Peter for the clothes to be picked up. We've all been under so much stress lately, with my husband passing and then this event, which has been in the planning for a year."

"I'm very sorry for your loss."

"Thank you. I'm happy to help out the church whenever I can. We've been having quite a time of it, trying to get ready for the fundraiser at the club. I thought we could wait until after to start clearing out some of my husband's belongings, but Bill thought it would be better to start right away, to keep me occupied so I don't dwell too much on things."

Mrs. Healey walked me over to a side room. It was an office, a long space with plenty of light streaming in. A big desk in the middle and built-in bookshelves around the walls that were crammed with books, photographs, trophies, various citations and other memorabilia.

"There are a couple of bags up here, then the rest are down in the garage." She saw that I was distracted, gawking at everything around me, the medals and photos and sense of accomplishment. "Quite impressive, don't you think?"

"Amazing."

She looked over the bags sadly. "Everything is in very good condition. Most of it was never even worn. People were always giving my husband things, hoping he would endorse their products. He never did, of course. He said it corrupted the game. I don't know why he held onto these clothes for so many years. I think it was in case anybody tried accusing him of taking gifts or bribes, or if there was trouble with the IRS. He kept very precise records."

I opened one of the bags and peeked inside. I saw some ugly pairs of polyester pants with the tags still on them. "Dead stock," I said. I saw the look on her face. "I'm sorry, that was an insensitive choice of words. *Dead stock* is a term for older clothes that have never been worn."

Her eyes went faraway.

"It wasn't insensitive at all. In fact, it's quite accurate. So much of our lives and experiences feel that way, like we've never taken the tags off them, or really given them a chance."

She leveled her gaze at me. Her eyes now had an empty sadness to them that I could not fathom. She spoke in even, calm tones.

"My husband's death was no accident. Nobody believes me, but I'm sure of it."

"May I ask why?"

"His putter is missing."

She looked at me as if this information was self-explanatory. I nodded vaguely. I didn't know what to say.

"I'll ask Dale to meet you down by the garage, to help with the rest. Excuse me." She turned without another word and exited through the far end of the office. I saw the big rude guy she had called Bill still skulking around the kitchen, giving me dirty looks.

I grabbed the bags and started out. I paused to look at some of the pictures. They were older photos, back when Corky was in his prime. For such a recluse he certainly ran with a powerful bunch. There was Corky with several presidents, going back to Truman and Eisenhower; there he was yukking it up with Bob Hope, Katharine Hepburn, Johnny Carson. There were other famous people but I couldn't read all the signatures.

The last few pictures I looked at were of Corky with a very young Mrs. Healey. She looked to be in her early twenties. She was beautiful now, but she had been a total knockout in her younger days. Corky must have been in his fifties by the time they met. A real stud. He was a handsome man, at least in the conventional sense, but there was something about his square jaw, big grin, and perpetual squint that I didn't quite like. In all the pictures his expression looked forced, or at the very least rehearsed. Maybe it was because of his intense privacy, I didn't know.

I dragged the bags outside and put them into the trunk of the Olds, then pulled around to the lower level of the house, by the garage. One of the doors was open and a younger guy was standing there, also in chinos and a polo shirt, eating a sandwich. I backed up the Olds, cut the engine and got out. The guy whistled.

"This your car?"

"Yes."

"442. Classic. Sixty-nine?"

"Eight."

That was pretty much all I knew about the car. That, and the fact that it was all original and in practically perfect condition. I had gotten it from an old lady whose lawn I used to mow every summer, every year from junior high through high school. The car had belonged to her husband, and when he died she said she wanted me to have it. She wanted five hundred dollars, which I knew was way too low, but she wouldn't take any more for it. And since I needed a car to get to and from college and couldn't afford much, I agreed. At the time the car had less than twenty thousand miles on it, and I had only put about another twenty on the original engine. Mrs. Dorgan had died a couple of years later, and I was thankful for that. If she had lived to see what had become of her favorite lawn boy, she would have been crushed. She was like a grandmother to me.

The guy stuck out his hand. "I'm Dale Healey."

"Bert. I'm sorry for your loss."

"Thanks. It's sad, but he wasn't exactly a spring chicken." Dale didn't take his eyes off the car. "Is this thing all original?"

"I think so."

"Mind if I check it out?"

"Be my guest."

Dale poked around under the hood while I got the bags. There were a lot of them, but the Olds has a big trunk. I shifted and turned them until they fit together. Dale oohed and aahed while he inspected the car. He examined the engine, the dashboard, the upholstery, under the carriage, everything. He even walked up the sloping driveway a bit, to look at it from a distance, then walked back down, shaking his head.

"Incredible. You ever think of selling her?"

"I almost did, once. But I'd never forgive myself if I did."

"Good man. Hold onto her. But if you ever change your mind, let me know."

"I will."

"Let me get the rest of the bags. I've been gawking so much that I haven't done anything."

Dale took the last remaining bags and squeezed them into the back seat. We had gotten so chummy over the car that I decided to press my luck.

"I don't mean to pry, but your mother said something before that I thought was strange."

"About my dad being the victim of foul play?"

I nodded. Dale looked up to the sky as he sighed. "I think mom is just having a hard time accepting the fact that he's gone. He was so youthful and energetic that I guess we all thought he would live forever. But he was ninety-one, for crying out loud."

"What makes her think there was foul play? I asked, but I didn't really understand."

"You're not the only one. What happened was, my dad was found at the bottom of the ravine, at the split fairway on the sixth. Do you know what I'm talking about?"

"No, sorry."

"On the sixth hole there's a wooded rough in the center of the fairway. In the middle of it there's a narrow ravine that leads down to a creek. It's not very big but it's steep, and if you get too close to the edge it would be easy to fall. They found him lying down there at the bottom with his 3-wood next to him. You see?" I shook my head. "Of course not. My mom says my dad never would have used a 3-wood for that shot."

"That's why she thinks he was murdered?"

"That, and the fact that his putter was missing from the bag. I admit that's a bit unusual. My dad might experiment with different clubs for different shots, but he wouldn't intentionally have gone without his favorite putter. It's very distinctive, with his name engraved on it."

"Maybe it fell out of the bag, or he left it at home?"

"No, we've checked all that. It's missing."

"So your mom thinks it was maybe used as a weapon?"

He raised his hands. "I guess so. But I don't know if my mom will ever be satisfied, to be honest. My dad devoted so much of his life to golf that I think she feels a little jealous, like he died in the arms of his true love, instead of at home in bed."

"I can understand that."

"Sure, to a point. But the fact is that we'll never know what my dad was thinking or planning when he slipped, and I don't think it matters. He was probably just retrieving a ball that landed too close to the edge of the ravine and he slipped."

"Maybe he was taking a leak."

Dale scowled at me. "My father wouldn't have relieved himself on the course."

"Sorry. I don't know anything about golf."

Dale shrugged. "Eh, it's all right. My father was a good man, he had plenty of friends and I don't think anyone killed him. Do you want something to drink?"

"Sure, thanks."

I followed Dale through the garage and into the house. My eyes hadn't adjusted from the bright sun to the darker basement hallway, but we soon came into a big room. Dale went over to a refrigerator in the corner and came back with two waters.

"This is the game room. I lived in here as a kid."

I motioned to the pool table in the center of the room. "Do you play?"

"Not really. My dad had that put in just a few months ago. He wanted to take pool lessons, if you can believe it. He knew he was becoming more frail and wouldn't be able to golf for much longer, so he wanted to master a new sport and win some tournaments if he could. Ninety-one years old and still competitive. Can you imagine?"

"Your dad sounds like a really cool guy."

He was. Not when you were playing against him, but otherwise, yeah, he was cool."

We stared at the table, drinking our waters in silence, until Dale spoke again. "When you spoke to my mom, did she mention that she's offering a reward to anyone who finds the putter?"

"No, she didn't mention that."

"Good. Maybe she's over it."

"No, I'm most certainly *not* over it."

Mrs. Healey was standing at the top of a stairway that led down to the game room, glaring at us both.

"I'd like to think that my own son wouldn't mock me for trying to protect his father, but I guess I was wrong. The reward still stands. Five hundred for the return of the putter, and five thousand for information leading to the arrest and conviction of the perpetrator. I think we're done here. Thank you for coming, young man. We need your help upstairs now, Dale."

Mrs. Healey turned sharply and disappeared. Behind her I caught another glimpse of the Bill guy. He looked angrier than ever, just a raging hard-on of hate. He gave me the serious creeps.

"I'm sorry," I said to Dale. "I didn't mean to get you in trouble."

"Not your fault at all. It was nice talking with you. Thanks for letting me check out your car."

Dale walked me back outside. He went over to the wall next to the garage and opened a little lid. There was a keypad. He punched a few numbers, stepped into the garage and a second later the door began sliding down. I started up the Olds and listened to her powerful engine with a new appreciation as she rumbled to life.

2112.

That was the code for the garage. It also happened to be the name of my favorite Rush album. I hadn't meant to look or be nosy but it wasn't like he was hiding it, either.

Now that I knew the code, my imagination went a bit wild. I thought of using it one night to sneak in on Mrs. Healey, lonely widow. I would tip-toe into her bedroom, drive her wild with pleasure and passion, and when it was over she would make me a ham sandwich.

The Olds bottomed out as I pulled out of the driveway. The engine had no trouble with the extra weight, but the shocks were a bit soft so I decided to take it slow. An old, beaten-up white van was behind me. He didn't seem to be in any more of a rush than I was, so I took it easy all the way to Mumfrey Boulevard, where I turned left and headed the last couple of miles to Bonnie's Bag.

Second

Bonnie's Bag is located in an old two-story house that sits on the edge of the St. Boniface parking lot. It was the former home of the people who had donated the property for the parish, which had once been farmland. The house is pretty rundown now, partly because the full-time caretaker for St. Boniface, who lives in the apartment above the store, is a drunk who is hardly ever around.

Outside of the parish there aren't too many people who know about Bonnie's Bag, which makes it one of the better thrift shops in town. As a teenager I used to scour the racks for my school clothes. I never dreamed that one day it would also be my office.

I rumbled across the empty lot and pulled around to the side entrance. The air was white with humidity, the trees lifeless, a hot, damp blanket smothering everything. I popped the trunk and dragged two bags inside.

"Where do you think you're going with those?"

Millie—or Millicent if she's in a bad mood, or Mrs. Devlin if she's really pissed off—is about eighty, hunched and frail, but she runs Bonnie's Bag with an iron fist, if you can imagine an iron fist that is shriveled and covered with age spots and big bulging purple veins. I stared at her, sweat pouring down my face.

"You can't drop anything off! We don't accept donations over the summer! Besides, we have no room!"

She was right, of course. The shop was already overflowing with old clothes, broken toys, incomplete puzzles, romance novels and costume jewelry. We had way more than we knew what to do with. That was part of the reason why Fr. Pete had hired me to help with the organizing and heavy lifting. I figured that if I played my cards right that I might outlast Millie and be promoted to manager when she croaked. It was something to shoot for.

Millie stood there, glaring at me, four and a half feet of righteous, wrinkled Irish fury.

"Well, are you just going to stand there with that dumb look on your face?"

"No. I'm just trying to figure out what to tell Fr. Peter, since he personally asked me to go to the Healey house for this stuff."

Millie's eyes widened.

"The Healeys? As in, Corky Healey?" I nodded. "Why didn't you say so? What are you doing just standing there? In you go! Make room in the back!"

Millie was happy now. As I dragged the first two bags into the storage room I heard her say out loud to herself, "Such a *handsome* man," and I know she wasn't talking about me.

I went into the storage room. It was filled with crap, but I saw where I could at least clear enough room for the new stuff. There was an old, sagging golf bag with a few clubs, standing in the corner. It looked like it had been there forever, but I checked it anyway. No putter. I went back to the Olds and dragged the other bags in. If the big, clock-like thermometer on the side of the thrift shop was to be believed, it was 90 degrees in the shade.

By the time I finished bringing in the bags I was soaking wet. I said good-bye to Millie, who was sitting behind the counter in the air conditioning, working on the *Daily News* crossword puzzle. She dismissed me with an impatient wave of her veiny hand.

I got into the Olds and leaned gently back against the burning vinyl. I wished I had been able to find out more from Mrs. Healey. I thought about stopping at the parish house to ask the Padre if he knew anything about it, but I was afraid he might ask me to do something else. It was supposed to be my day off, and I still had a bag of laundry to do and several cold beers to toss back.

I could check around at the other thrift shops. It was a million to one shot, but if I could find that putter it meant five bills, which would be a huge help. I didn't think seriously about finding a killer, because I believed Dale that there wasn't one. Otherwise I'd probably confess, just to claim the reward.

As I pulled away I noticed that the parking lot was no longer empty. There was a white van parked halfway between the thrift shop and the school. It looked like the van I saw in Pondington, but I couldn't tell for sure. The plates weren't local. I leaned forward in the seat to avoid the burning black vinyl upholstery, and started off for the Slosh.

The Slosh 'n Wash sits in a sad little strip mall down on lower Shore Road, in the part of Mumfrey that's as close to working class as a town like Mumfrey can get. I started going there after moving into the rooming-house. The place is a dive, but it has several advantages. First, it is the closest bar to my room, which means I can walk to and from it without having to worry about getting a DWI, which would be especially bad for me. Second, whoever built the Slosh had the brilliant idea of putting a row of washers and dryers along the back wall, making it either the world's coolest Laundromat or most practical bar, depending on how you looked at it. Third, and probably most importantly, there is Ruby.

Ruby moved up to Mumfrey from some dusty little town in west Texas a few years ago with some boyfriend, who got her pregnant and then left before she even had the baby. The cad went back to Texas, but Ruby stayed. That was a lucky break for us slobs who hang out at the Slosh, because Ruby is a fiery, ginger-haired goddess, about as beautiful and exotic a creature as you're likely to find in these parts.

Every guy is in love with her, including me, but there's a catch. Ruby has a kid. Her name is Chanel, and she's four years old and a piece of work. She looks just like Ruby and has twice the sass. Some guys go for that pre-made family thing but I'm in no position to get into something like that when I can't even take care of myself. And who knows if or when the boyfriend is going to decide to come back and demand to see his kid. It's like a bad country song waiting to happen, and I can't afford to get into any more trouble. Lucky for me I don't like country music very much.

I pulled in next to Ruby's red Wrangler, and dragged my laundry inside. Ruby was poured into a pair of skin tight Levi's, expertly faded, and had a checkered blouse tied around her midriff, showing off her flat belly and navel ring. Her hair looked like a waterfall of fire, if that makes sense, and she had the sweetest Texas accent to go with it. She gave me a big smile, then noticed the bag and made a sad face.

"I thought you loved me, Bert Shambles, but all I am is a big bunch of washing machines to you."

"I told you, Ruby, any time you want to go for a spin cycle with me, just let me know."

"Need quarters, hon? The change machine is broken."

"Thanks." I handed over a five.

"HEY BERT."

I jumped. It was Oscar. Oscar doesn't talk, he YELLS. I can't get used to it, but I can put up with it because he's such a genuinely nice person. I met him when I first started coming to the Slosh a few months back, shortly after the trial ended. I don't know how old he is, but he looks older than he seems. He has some gray starting to show up in his long black hair, which is always pulled back in a ponytail. He wears extremely thick glasses that don't seem to help, since he still keeps the books he's always reading pushed right up to his nose. Oscar lives with his mom, and I don't think he has ever held a job. He is in the Slosh almost every day, drinking Coke, reading books, and sometimes stopping to play Yahtzee with Ruby or some of the other regulars. I like him a lot.

The door to the Slosh opened. The glare from outside was too bright to see who it was. I rubbed my eyes and took a drink, thinking it might help. It didn't. The guy who had just arrived went down to the far end of the bar, slapped a bill on the counter and asked for change. He had an accent that was similar to Ruby's. He even called her *darlin'*.

I glanced over at the guy and immediately wished I hadn't. He was looking right at me, staring, with as mean and ugly a face as I'd ever seen.

Red hair and freckles can go either way—when they're done right, like with Ruby, they are the sexiest, most beautiful things in the world. This guy had inherited the other kind. His hair was wild and stuck out all over. His skin was sickly pale and splotched with large clumps of freckles, his teeth were long and brown. But what freaked me out more than the face itself was the expression on it: he had a sneering, slit-eyed kind of mug that was instantly unlikeable. He would have been tall even without cowboy boots, and was wiry and muscular. In my mind I called him Carrot Top, because there was nothing funny about him.

"WHAT HAVE YOU BEEN UP TO, BERT?"

I jumped again. And I could see in the mirror behind the bar that Carrot Top jumped too. He muttered under his breath and started separating and counting the quarters.

"Not much. I had to do a pick-up for work. We got a big donation from Corky Healey's wife."

"THE GOLF PLAYER?"

"The very same."

"I heard about that," Ruby said. "So sad. Didn't he fall down a hole or something?"

"Ravine. The split fairway on six."

"How do you know so much about it?"

"I'm actually investigating something for Mrs. Healey," I said. "She thinks there was foul play, including a missing golf club. She asked me to look into it for her."

Ruby's eyes flashed. "Really? You're a private investigator now? That is so exciting!"

It was an exaggeration, sure, maybe even a lie, but I loved giving Ruby the impression that there was more to me than there actually was. She was one of the few people who hadn't judged me for getting into trouble with the law. I don't know if that's because I had defended a woman's honor or because Ruby's from the South, and is therefore used to people she knows spending time in jail.

Ruby leaned over the bar and whispered. "Do you really think he was murdered?"

"Hard to say. Not enough information yet."

"If you find out anything juicy you'd better let me know, Sherlock."

"What do I get in return?"

"What do you want?"

"I'd like to find out if your hair is your natural color."

She snapped a bar rag at me.

We were startled by a slamming sound, of a hand on the bar counter. I looked over at Carrot Top; he was glaring at me.

"You all right?" Ruby had an edge in her voice.

"Just gettin' my change," he drawled, dragging the quarters off the bar. He shot me a look. "That okay with you, Sherlock?" Then he walked to the back and put the quarters in the pool table, and started noisily racking up a new game. The guy had a bad vibe and we all felt it: Ruby went over to the stereo behind the bar and flipped through the CDs, as if looking for an antidote; Oscar was involving himself in whatever Sci-Fi epic he was reading, with his nose firmly in the crease between the pages.

I got up to use the bathroom. As I went in, I could see in my peripheral vision that Carrot Top was standing still, staring at me. I could feel his evil yellow eyes burning into me. I locked the door, just in case, and was careful coming out, but a brief glance over my shoulder as I headed back to the bar confirmed that Carrot Top was now more interested in practicing his pool shots.

Whatever the guy's problem was, he seemed to be over it, so I took my quarters and dragged the laundry bag to the back. I went over to the detergent dispenser and started feeding it.

"Looks like they'll let any scumbag in this place." It was Carrot Top again. His voice was a hiss, dripping with mockery. "I can't imagine being such a piece of alcoholic white trash that I'd go to a bar to do my wash." He pronounced it *warsh*.

I felt a knot in my stomach. I couldn't understand why he was picking on me, like some schoolyard bully. As if Long Island didn't have enough assholes; now we were importing them from out of state.

I did what Dr. K would have recommended, and focused my Third Eye on the Rainbow of Understanding, while still feeding my quarters into the soap machine—slowly, one at a time, so they wouldn't jam.

A pool cue poked me in the back. I dropped a quarter on the floor, and it rolled under one of the machines.

"You think you're pretty slick, don't you?"

"Look, man, I don't want any trouble."

I still had my back to the guy. Carrot Top came up behind me and spoke softly into my ear. His breath smelled like cold cuts and gum disease.

"Of course you don't, fagot. But that's what you got."

I pulled the lever, got the box of soap. I decided laundry could wait. I picked up the bag and started back to the bar.

"That's right, fagot, run away. You ain't a man if you need some dirty skank like that bitch to protect you."

I stopped in my tracks.

This was a problem. You can insult me all you want, but when you insult a woman I care about—well, that's what got me into trouble in the first place. Still, I couldn't control myself. I turned slowly and grinned.

(Doctor Kornbluth, if you're reading this, you might want to skip ahead a few pages.)

I'll spare you the details of exactly what I said. What I told the guy, in so many words, was that he should perform fellatio on me and/or engage in sexual activity with his own person. I then referred to his mother as a female dog, and implied that he was the product of a fatherless union. I continued by making disparaging remarks about his hair color and accent, and implied that he came from a region where intra-family breeding is not only the norm but encouraged, and urged him to get back to the loving arms of his sister as soon as possible, etc. You get the idea.

Yes, he started it, but yes, I'm an idiot. I finished my little speech and, feeling quite pleased with myself, turned and walked coolly to my seat. Or I should say, walked *toward* the seat. I never actually made it. The last thing I remember was a dull, sickening crack against my shoulders and head, and then I was floating softly down to the ground.

Then

A Saint Bernard was chasing a marshmallow ambulance through fields of giant sunflowers. It was raining watering cans. Two mice danced on a faraway cloud.

I was peering down a great abyss, a yawning chasm opening into black infinity. I was dead. Not only was I dead, but I was descending into hell.

Something glittered at me from the depths of the canyon, the distant fires of eternal torment. My eyes struggled to focus. I saw Satan. No, Jesus. He was shining like the rays of the sun, hanging from a cross of gold.

Judgment Day.

"Take me, Jesus!" I cried, and ran after him. The ground was soft and spongy and smelled sweet. If this was hell then I was going to like it. Then Jesus spoke.

"Hey! What do you think you're doing?"

Fuzzy stars blinked on and off. Stabs of light, bursts of random noise and activity like a radio dial being spun. A giant pair of shoes.

I was aware of being on my back, and the stars morphed into faces. The world was cold. I was on the floor. Hospital? Paralyzed? I thought very hard, then the pointer finger on my right hand twitched. I tried to move the rest of me but everything was limp and putty-like.

The mountains receded. Jesus and the cross were hanging on a golden rope. Illusion. I looked up. Hell had a drop ceiling that was badly in need of a cleaning.

"Get back, everybody, he's coming to!"

My eyes focused a little more and my brain rebooted. I was in Ruby's arms. A gold crucifix dangled from a chain around her neck. The smelly mountains were the soft, fragrant mounds of flesh pressed together in that gingham shirt. She helped me into a sitting position and I rubbed my eyes.

"What happened?"

"YOU STUCK YOUR NOSE IN RUBY's BOOBS!" Oscar bellowed. Ruby shushed him.

"Give him some room. Bert, are you all right?"

"I don't know. What happened?"

"You got whacked with a pool cue. Can you get up, hon?

"Depends. Which way is it?"

Ruby held me under one arm and Oscar grabbed the other and together they hoisted me back onto my feet and over to a stool.

"I was going to call 911," Ruby said, "but Oscar reminded me that you had a little trouble with the law, and we didn't want you to get into more trouble. Sorry. I can call them now if you want."

"No, thank you. It was the right thing to not do."

"YOU SHOULD STILL GO TO THE HOSPITAL AND GET AN X-RAY. YOU MIGHT HAVE A CONCUSSION."

"What are the symptoms?"

"DIZZY SPELLS, BLACK OUTS, CONFUSION."

"In that case I've had a concussion for the last ten years."

"Don't make jokes, Bert! This is really serious. You could have been killed."

Ruby went behind the bar and put some ice in a towel for me, which I held against my neck, then set me up with a beer and a shot. I was feeling steadier. Ruby was obsessively wiping down the area of the bar in front of me, as if it might help.

One thought kept going through my head: I had pressed my face into her breasts. I was pretty psyched about that. I put my hand on Ruby's to make her stop the obsessive wiping.

"You ever seen that guy before?"

"He looks familiar. He might have been in here once or twice. Only recently, though. He's not from around here. He's from Louisiana."

"Did he tell you that?"

"No. I remember his license from when I carded him. He drives a nasty old van."

"What color?"

"I don't know."

"IT's WHITE."

"Oh yeah, that's right. But dirty. And real beat up. Bert, why did you even start with that guy?"

"As I recall, he started with me."

"I know, hon, but you should just ignore people like that."

"I disagree. It's my civic duty to tell assholes what I think of them. If we all did maybe there wouldn't be so many of them around."

"OR MAYBE THAT'S WHAT EVERYBODY ELSE DOES SO THAT'S WHY PEOPLE ARE RUDE ALL THE TIME."

Ruby's expression changed. For a beautiful woman she can sometimes have a hard look about her, like she's seen too much, or been lied to too much, or had too many promises broken. She's the type of girl that country-western singers write achy-breaky songs about, but I couldn't tell yet if the song would have a happy or sad ending. Meanwhile, she smiled that beautiful smile and touched my hand.

"I heard what he said about me and how you stuck up for me. That was sweet of you. Thanks, darling. Drinks are on me tonight."

Ruby had some aspirin in her purse, and I took two. She set me up with a beer and a shot, then another. I figured I might as well enjoy the sympathy while it lasted.

It had to be the same van.

It was dark out by the time I realized I had to go or I'd never make it. My neck was getting very stiff, and I was pretty drunk. Ruby came around and helped me to my feet.

"Are you okay to drive?"

"No way. I'll just lock the laundry in the car and walk home."

"I'LL DRIVE YOU HOME, BERT."

Oscar had driven me home once before. He is the ultimate bar buddy, since he doesn't drink alcohol. He once told me that he goes to the Slosh for the companionship. His mother does his laundry.

Ruby scribbled her number on a napkin and shoved it into my hand. Next to the number she had drawn a heart. She hugged me.

"You take care of yourself, tiger. Call me if you need me."

"Thanks, Ruby. I'm sorry for smelling your boobs."

Oscar carried my laundry bag out to the car and fit it into the back seat of his rusted Corolla, then I carefully got into the passenger seat. The car was filled with paperbacks and empty Burger King bags. My neck and back were stiffening up nicely. I had a welt the size of a golf ball on the back of my skull, and another one growing somewhere between my neck and right shoulder.

We started to my place. Oscar took it easy on the drive, up the long winding road past the vocational school, the strip mall with the Chinese take-out and convenience store, the sad little place with bars on the windows where you could buy cheap gold, send money via Western Union, and get payday advances at loan-shark rates.

On the other side of the street was the cemetery. It was so quiet in there, so big and peaceful, filled with other people who couldn't get off Long Island. I wondered if that would be my fate, if I was destined to beat my head against the watery bars of a floating prison until I croaked.

"Left here."

We turned off the main drag, then veered right at the fork, then a quick, sharp right up my steep dead-end street, Cheshire Lane. The rooming-house was at the top, second house from the end on the right. The little Corolla struggled but we made it.

"WHO'S THAT?"

It was dark and I had trouble focusing. For a second I was gripped with fear that it might be Carrot Top, but in the weak beams of the headlights I could see a dark-haired guy leaning against a sedan in front of the rooming-house. I groaned.

"It's my probation officer. Relax, I'll handle this."

Daddy-O came over and leaned into the window. Real cool cat. Mustache. Stupid hair. Gold chain. Masculine scent.

"There you are, Shambles. Mind if I talk to you for a few minutes?"

"Do I have a choice?"

"Not really. Who's your friend?"

Oscar was staring straight ahead. He looked terrified.

"This is Oscar. Say hello to Officer Paul D'Addario, Oscar."

Oscar squeaked out something unintelligible.

"Your friend okay? He on drugs or something?"

"He's fine. Drinks only Coca-Cola."

"Maybe you should try that sometime."

I climbed out of the Corolla, dragged the bag from the back and patted the hood. "Thanks for the ride."

Oscar turned the car around slowly on the empty street, painstakingly, using his blinkers and his hands to signal each move. He acted like his only mission in life was to obey every single traffic law ever invented, on earth or any other planet in the universe, now and forever. He was awesome.

Daddy-O and I started up the walk. Privately I call him Daddy-O, but never to his face. I have to meet with Officer D'Addario once a month, at his office in downtown Brooklyn. I've only met with him a few times so far. When I moved to the rooming-house I notified him of my new address, as I'm required to, and now he was finally checking up on me.

"What's in the bag?"

"Heroin."

"Funny."

"Laundry."

"You're walking funny. Are you all right?"

"I pulled a muscle at work."

Daddy-O looked up at the rooming-house. It had been built back in the 1930s or so, and had not been updated or renovated since. Peeling tar paper, crumbling roof, missing panes here and there. Even the long, brown and dead grass seemed to keep growing, like hair on a corpse. I got the door open and we headed upstairs.

"This place is pretty run down. Why don't you live at your mom's house?"

"Why don't you?"

"All right, I get it. How much did you drink tonight?"

"My probation does not prohibit me from consuming alcohol."

"No, but it does prohibit you from busting my balls."

He had me there. We made it upstairs. I got the flimsy lock open, pushed the creaking door and turned on the overhead light, an old fixture with only one of the three bulbs working. I dropped the bag in the corner and Daddy-O came in, slowly, looking around with a pained expression.

"*This* is where you're living?"

"It's all I can afford. Have a seat."

I cleared the chair for Daddy-O. I sat on the edge of the cot. He looked at the typewriter on the desk.

"You a writer?"

"No. My anger-management counselor thought it would be a good idea for me to keep a journal."

"How is it going?"

"I don't know, I just started. Don't worry, there's nothing about you. Not yet, anyway."

Daddy-O smiled at this, then pulled a notepad and pen from his sport coat. It was too hot to be wearing a jacket but he didn't seem to be sweating at all. He opened to a page and started writing. I sat on the cot, not saying anything. I looked at the floor: a few empty beer bottles, half-full jug of water, loose papers. A small black and white television that I bought for five bucks at Bonnie's Bag. The antenna is broken so it only picks up a handful of channels, including PBS and two Spanish stations. I watch a lot of nature programs and *Sábado Gigante*.

"What's your rent here?"

"Seventy-five a week."

Daddy-O scribbled in the pad. "Do you have a girlfriend?"

"Not at the moment."

"Seeing anyone? Nobody?"

I shook my head.

"Doing any drugs? Hiding anything in here that you shouldn't be hiding?"

"I don't believe in drugs," I said. "But you're welcome to search the place."

"I don't think that will be necessary. Are you still employed?"

"Yes. I work at St. Boniface, mostly in the thrift shop, but I do other odd jobs as needed."

Daddy-O made a few more scribbles and then closed the notebook. "Look, Bert. I'll be honest with you. I see a lot of guys like you. Angry, resentful. They feel like they got a bad rap so they take it out on the world. I'm not here to tell you how to live, but I see you living in a place like this, you've been drinking, you're wising off, and I worry that it's not going to end well for you. Understand what I'm saying?"

"I think so."

"Good. Because I want you to succeed."

"Thanks."

"Are you socializing? Meeting people? Meeting girls?"

"Not yet, but I'd like to."

"How about your former girlfriend? Do you ever contact her?"

"No. I haven't spoken to her since the trial. She told me that she never wanted to see me again, and that if I contacted her she would consider it harassment. Why, has she been claiming that I've contacted her?"

"No, nothing like that. I'm just asking."

He stood up and extended a hand. I got up with some difficulty and we shook.

"Like I said, I'm not going to bother searching your room. But watch your drinking, and stay out of trouble."

"Yes sir."

"And see a doctor about that pulled muscle. You look like hell."

I went to the window and watched as Daddy-O got into his compact sedan and pulled away. He wasn't a bad guy, not really. But he was still a cop, or semi-cop, or whatever the hell probation officers are, and that meant he represented authority and courts, judges and lawyers. He was part of a system that was only designed for one purpose, to grind people like me into hamburger meat, and I wanted nothing more to do with any of it.

I was so stiff from pain and tension that I could barely get myself undressed. I crawled under the sheet on the cot and was asleep in about five minutes. The last thing I remember thinking was a phrase that kept looping in my head, over and over:

My life sucks.

And then

By the morning my neck had spasmed into a solid fist of pain so powerful that my right ear was welded to my shoulder. It was an unbelievable pain, absurd and tragic. I gingerly reached for the jug of water on the floor by the bed and the bottle of aspirin on the radiator. I took two tablets and several big gulps of water as great flashes of agony shot through my upper body, then carefully turned myself over and lay back down on the cot. And then, I'm not ashamed to admit it, I began to cry.

I deserved it. Me, the almost-killer. My troubles would never be over, I would never be able to live down the consequences of what I had done. Because my heart was not pure and never would be.

I reached up and felt the giant welt that had formed, a big tender lump about the size of an egg. I couldn't wait for the aspirin to take effect; I needed ice. I crawled over to the little fridge. The ice tray compartment was completely frozen over, covered in a thick coat of icy fuzz. I tried scraping some of the fuzz with my fingertips, then a plastic spoon. No use. I got into a semi-sitting position and leaned my head back until the lump made contact with the ice.

When you're down and out, things that go right can get exaggerated in your mind. I was lying on a sticky, dirty floor in a tiny, filthy room, pushing my injured head into a crummy dorm fridge, but suddenly I felt like Rockefeller relaxing on his yacht. I had it made.

Then I smelled something foul.

It was the smell of death—or worse, rotting cauliflower––multiplied by a thousand dead zombies floating in a sewage treatment plant. After a little more investigation I realized the smell was coming from me. In fact, it *was* me. I badly needed a hot shower and to get out of my clothes. I remembered with a groan that I hadn't done my laundry. I would have to get at least one more day of use out of them. I walked the fingers of my left hand across the floor, grabbed hold of the plastic garbage bag and dragged it over. I reached into the bag and pulled out a pair of pants.

They were bright pink, with green whales on them.

I reached in again. This time I pulled out a bright orange knit vest with blue golf clubs stitched all around it. I kept pulling out items. Instead of my familiar gray work pants and black T-shirts, I removed a steady stream of insane sweaters, barf-ugly shirts and deranged pants, all done in various argyles and checks, stripes and polka dots, in an assortment of fabrics that had been grown in laboratories by self-hating petroleum engineers. It was the ugliest junk I had ever laid eyes on.

I leaned my head back onto the ice compartment and tried to remember. I knew for a fact that I had put the laundry next to me on the front seat when I had left the house. I replayed the events of the day until I remembered: the car. Dale Healey had been so anxious to check out the Olds that at one point he had gone into the passenger side to look at something, the dash or the upholstery or maybe the glove compartment. He must have moved my bag off the seat, thinking it was one of the donated bags of clothing, and then put a different bag there when he helped me at the end. I had been so flattered by his interest, and so distracted by the other bags, that I hadn't noticed. He had put a bag back on the front seat, all right, except it wasn't my laundry.

That meant that my clothes were now sitting in the storage room at Bonnie's Bag, and I was the proud owner of a dead man's collection of fluorescent polyester golfing outfits. Wonderful.

It wasn't like my clothes were any good—they weren't––but they were all I had, except maybe for some old things at my mom's house. I didn't have the money to buy a new wardrobe, and there was no way in hell I was going to start wearing powder blue pants with yellow golf carts embroidered on them, or a shiny 1970s polo shirt with a photo print of a sunset wrapped around it. Or how about those loud, green-and-white checked polyester bell bottoms in a hideous waffle weave? You like them? Fine, you wear them.

I took some deep breaths and built a bridge to my happy place. Tried changing the things I couldn't accept, or however it goes.

It was simple, really. I would go to Bonnie's Bag and make the switch. After some more thought I decided that it would be better to be in clean and ugly clothes than the stinking things I had on, so I rooted through the bag for something to wear. Based on the general style of the stuff, as well as the lettering on the labels, along with the complete and utter absence of any natural fibers whatsoever, I guessed the clothes were mostly from the late 60s or early 70s.

As you can probably tell, I actually do know a little about clothes. Especially vintage clothing. For a while I even considered a career in fashion, and I still regret not going to FIT. I've shopped in thrift shops most of my life, out of necessity, and eventually I got good at it, able to spot good pieces that I could sell for a profit to some of the vintage places in the city. There's a place in Brooklyn that I still bring stuff to once in a while, but Cassie wouldn't want this stuff.

When it comes to vintage clothing, like with anything else, not all pieces are created equal. Maybe a collector of vintage golf clothes somewhere in California or Florida would love to get his hands on such a collection, but that didn't do me any good. I don't have a digital camera, computer, or internet access, so I can't really sell the stuff on Ebay unless I figure out a way to upload it using one of the public computers at the library, which is too much of a hassle.

I got up with a lot of difficulty and took a shower. My bath towel was in the laundry bag so I used my bed sheet instead. I didn't have any clean underwear so I put the old pair of boxer briefs back on, then found a not terrible pair of lightweight powder blue pants with yellow golf carts on them, and a slippery, bright orange short-sleeve golf shirt, the tag of which claimed it was "100% Genuine Silk Feel." The good news was that old Corky had roughly the same build as me. I looked like a clown, but at least I was a clean, well-tailored clown.

In my condition it was hard to get the bag of golf clothes down the stairs, but I managed. It wasn't until I got outside that I remembered that the Olds was still down at the Slosh. It was almost a mile walk, and it was a blisteringly hot morning already. I cursed, dragged the bag back upstairs, locked it in my room, then started off a second time for the Slosh. I was already sweaty and exhausted and I hadn't even left the house.

I made it to Route 59, which would take me back down past the cemetery and to the Slosh, there for all the world to see in my cheery pants and blinding shirt. My body throbbed with every slow, agonizing step. A cute girl riding with some friends yelled "I like your style!" A minute later, a couple of young men blew kisses at me, and another called me an asshole and gave me the finger. A plastic soda bottle whizzed by my head.

Did I mention how much I hate Long Island?

I heard a shout. The voice came from across the street. I looked over toward the direction of the sound and the blood drained out of my body. A beat-up white van was stopped in the opposite lane. The angry face snarling back at me was more horrible than I remembered.

I hobbled for it. The mummy shuffle, going nowhere fast. The only bit of good luck was that traffic was heavy, so Carrot Top couldn't make a U-turn. Cars were piling up behind him and, in true Long Island fashion, the drivers began a chorus of angry honks and curses. Carrot Top floored it. There was a left-turn lane just up the road at the next corner; the van swerved over and waited for an opening.

There was no time to think. I cut up Dakota Street, which runs through a residential area. I went left, then right, zig-zagging my way deeper into the subdivision. I was in too much pain to run, but I kind of hop-skipped as fast as I could. I ducked every time I heard an engine. The first couple were false alarms, but the third time I crouched behind a car I peeked through the rear window and saw the white van race down the street. It had taken Carrot Top a few minutes to turn that boat around and come after me, so he probably thought I had gotten much farther than I had.

I didn't see the van again. I kept vigilant and stayed low until I made it to Shore Road, across from the sad little strip mall that is home to the Slosh. The bar wasn't open yet, but luckily the Olds was still there. I cranked the windows open to let out some of the heat, then put her into drive and maneuvered onto the road, scanning constantly for the van. I got back to the house, went upstairs and got the bag. Then I went into the closet and grabbed the vintage stuff that I had been collecting for my next trip to Brooklyn. I didn't really have enough to justify the gas I would burn going there and back, but I had decided that it was a good day for a road trip, in case Carrot Top was still out there, looking for me.

I was about to leave the room for my third time that morning when something caught my eye. The sun was streaming in through my tattered, ripped curtains; something glinted from the desk. It was a gold pen, sitting next to my typewriter. A Cross. Not a very expensive item, but nicer than anything I owned. It looked like the pen that Daddy-O used.

Great. The guy was probably already getting a search warrant and SWAT team together to raid my place. The pen was an excuse for him to come back and make a surprise search when he thought he could catch me off-guard, doing something illegal. I saw a documentary on PBS once about a type of fish that does something similar, by dangling a little piece of skin in front of its face, like bait on a pole.

I put the pen in my pocket. Daddy-O's offices weren't too far from where the vintage shop was, so I decided to swing by and return it while I was in the area. I didn't like all the stuff he said about me being angry and on the edge, the questions about Devil Girl. It had almost sounded like a threat. Maybe this would earn me some brownie points with him.

I dragged the bag of clothes across the overgrown yard and pushed it into the Olds and was off in a matter of seconds. My heart was racing, but at least the adrenaline relieved the pain a little. At the bottom of my street I made a quick left and stopped at the three-way intersection, just as the battered van turned off of Route 59 and headed my way. I had just enough time to duck; the van rumbled past without pausing.

I got back to St. Boniface and dragged the bag out of the car, nearly in tears. The adrenaline had worn off and with the heat and stress and exertion the pain was back to being ridiculous. Millie gave me her patented look of Celtic disgust.

"No more donations! I don't care it's from the Pope himself!" Her expression changed from anger to shock. "Why on earth are you wearing that ridiculous outfit?"

I explained about the mix-up and told her that I had to get my own clothes back. Millie shook her head defiantly.

"You can't do that."

Now this was too much, even by Millie's standards. I tried to stay calm by remembering that she was an old lady, and most likely a widow. Then I remembered that most old ladies are widows because they put their husbands into early graves, and I got mad all over again.

"Look," I said sharply. "Those are my only clothes, and as it is I had to wear this ridiculous get-up just to get here. If you're going to be difficult about it then I'll have to go over your head."

Millie sniffed, unimpressed. "See what I care," she said again. "You can't have them back. They're gone."

"What do you mean?"

"He picked them up already."

"Who?"

"Mr. Healey's son. He came by this morning. He said there had been a mistake and that he needed the clothes back. Go look for yourself if you don't believe me." She picked up her pencil and went back to the crossword puzzle.

She was senile, she had to be. I went back to the storage room. It was like she said, the clothes were gone. I walked back to the front in a daze. Millie spoke in a sarcastic, sing-song kind of voice without looking up.

"Did you find what you were looking for?"

I didn't respond. I had to talk to the Padre. I dragged the bag of golf clothes behind me, unable to lift them any more.

I drove to the other side of the parking lot, to the back entrance of the church. I thought that I probably qualified for the handicapped spot by the door, but a big, shiny new Cadillac was already there. I went in and heard some voices coming from the main room. I cut through the sacristy and stood by the open doorway, out of sight. The Padre was standing in the center aisle, near the altar, talking with some customers.

Tough customers, by the looks of it. A big, beefy guy in a shiny suit. A woman who I took to be his wife, and two younger women. The first looked just like the older woman, so I figured it was a daughter. They were both large, homely women. The other one was a different story: she was tiny, petite, and absolutely gorgeous.

I never believed in love at first sight, all that junk about cupid with his bow and arrow, until that moment. I could actually feel the arrow hit me, though it might have been just another neck spasm. Either way, that's what happened when I saw her. If you had asked me before that moment to describe my perfect woman I would have told you the truth, that I would know her when I saw her. Well, I had just seen her. She had long, straight dark hair that went partly down her back; her skin was beautifully tan, her teeth white, her body soft and hard, straight and round in all the exactly right places. I was standing there, frozen, when something incredible happened. She turned and looked right at me. And then she smiled. Not a polite smile, either, but a long, lingering look, the kind of look that makes you feel as if you've just been clobbered on the back of the head by a pool cue. It was a glowing, radiant kind of a smile that seemed to last forever. I was so shocked that I checked to see if she was smiling at someone standing behind me. There was nobody else.

I pulled my head back and hid behind the doorway, breathing hard. Then I walked carefully back into the sacristy, sat down and tried to catch my breath.

After that

When his meeting was over Father Pete came breezing into the sacristy. He was in good spirits, as usual. He's a tall man, and nice looking for a priest, with a square face, big glasses, and salt and pepper hair.

"Bert! What a nice surprise. How did it go at the Healeys, yesterday?"

Father Pete noticed my outfit and blinked, then shook his head as if he had imagined it. I explained what happened, including the mix-up and how the clothes had been taken back by the Healeys. The Padre listened intently.

"Very strange, indeed. Mrs. Healey was quite anxious to get the clothing out of the house."

"What should I do?"

"Hard to say. People aren't always thinking clearly in such times; sometimes they have regrets. Would you like me to call Dorothy and ask her about it?"

In fact I wanted nothing more, but Father Pete had done enough for me already. I had to prove to myself that I wasn't completely dependent on others to get me out of problems that I created for myself.

"I think I'll just run over there and explain what happened."

Fr. Pete nodded. "That sounds very sensible. I'm sure it's just an honest mix-up. If you have any more problems, let me know. Can you still take care of things here after the Tortura wedding tomorrow?"

"Of course. Why wouldn't I?"

"I don't know, you seem to be moving a little stiffly. Did you hurt yourself?"

"Just slept kind of funny. I'm fine."

"Four o'clock?"

"See you then. By the way, was that the wedding family you were meeting with just now?"

"Yes. I was speaking with the bride and her parents, and the maid of honor."

"She's going to be a beautiful bride."

Fr. Pete looked up at the wall with a thoughtful expression.

"You really think so? I'd think the younger sister would be more your type." Fr. Pete gave me a knowing smile. "And yes, Bert, as far as I know she's still single."

By the time I got back to the Healey house I was almost going to miss the crazy clothes. They had a certain charm, in an ugly kind of way. It was definitely a unique look. They worked even better with the Olds, too, since they were both around the same age.

I pulled up the banked, semi-circular driveway, went up and rang the bell. Mrs. Healey answered.

"Yes?"

I was about to speak when she got a look on her face that I will not soon forget. Shock, horror, and disgust rolled into one unforgettable package.

"Are you wearing my dead husband's clothes?"

"Mrs. Healey, I can explain. There was a mix-up. My laundry bag got in with your donation. So I'm here to return your clothes and get mine back."

"You're what?"

The look on her face really freaked me out.

"Returning these?"

"I cannot believe this is happening."

"But Millie at the thrift shop said that Dale picked them up again."

"Dale? Dale is in London on business for a few days."

"But Millie said—"

The door slammed in my face.

Now, as foolish as I might be, can you at least understand why I sometimes get the feeling that the whole world is against me? I limped back to the car, groaning. Stylish, ha. These stupid rags were becoming a real pain in the ass.

The problem, as always, was money. I could buy some things at the thrift shop to hold me over, but I still had to buy a lot of new stuff: socks, underwear, bath towel. That stuff added up quick, even at Sears or JC Penney. It was more than I could afford at the moment. I hoped the few vintage pieces I had collected over the past few months would earn me enough to hold me over until payday. I turned the Olds around and started for Brooklyn.

Cassie's Closet is on Bedford Avenue, in the heart of Williamsburg. It's the kind of neighborhood where I should be living, except I don't know how anyone but stockbrokers and drug dealers can afford it. My hope was that at the end of my probation I could still sell the Olds for a good amount, maybe get a job in the city and then I would live in a neighborhood like that. Or maybe I'd move to Hawaii and open an ice cream shop. Maybe Seattle, or Mexico. I had plenty of time to decide, and in the meantime I wasn't going anywhere.

I took the LIE to the BQE, then just over the Kosciusko bridge I took the exit that brought me up to Bedford Avenue. I found a parking spot around the corner, grabbed the vintage stuff and hoped for the best.

Cassie has one of the best vintage places in the city, and pays well for good pieces: forty percent of retail, cash on the spot. She runs a thriving business while also putting extra money into the pocket of anyone with quality merchandise.

The bell on the door jingled as I entered. Cassie's old hound, Jasper, was resting his droopy lips on his front paws near the entrance. He stood up when I came in and began sniffing my crotch, then followed me to the counter. A moment later Cassie pushed through the bead curtain in the back.

Cassie looks kind of plain at first glance, with light brown hair that she keeps short and choppy, and a soft feminine chin and calm, light brown eyes. Even though she has some of the best vintage clothes in the city, she dresses very modestly, almost boyishly. Cassie isn't the kind of girl who will make heads snap when she walks into a room, but once you get to know her, watch her for a while, and see how graceful and put-together she really is, you realize she's a total babe.

"Bert! How have you been? It seems like forever." Cassie stopped and her face fell. "*What* are you wearing?"

I rolled my eyes and laughed. "Long story. It's all I have at the moment. I look ridiculous."

Cassie was smiling, shaking her head. She took a big crunch out of an apple and spoke with her mouth full, which was another endearing quality about her.

"Ridiculous? You look...amazing."

"Don't make fun, please. It's been a rough couple of days."

"I'm not making fun! Are you kidding? Vintage golf clothes are the hottest thing going right now. It's impossible to find good stuff, because it's so out of left field, nobody ever stocked it before. Where did you find those?"

"They were a donation, to the thrift shop where I work."

"I'd buy them right off your back if I could."

I was about to let it slide, then I thought about it. The Padre didn't care one way or the other, Mrs. Healey wanted nothing to do with them, and Millie only wanted to give me a hard time. Why should I care?

"I've got a bag in the car, if you want to take a look."

Her eyes widened. "Bring them in!"

I went out to retrieve the bag. As soon as I stepped onto Bedford Avenue a cute young woman smiled at me and said hi. I went from being the world's biggest dork to feeling like the coolest guy in town. Looking like that would get me beaten up in Mumfrey, but in Williamsburg it would get me a date. Probation couldn't be over soon enough.

Cassie's eyes bugged when she saw the size of the bag. She cleared off the counter and started pulling things out as fast as she could. There was a golfing cap with a pompom on it in the bag, knitted with the colors of the Irish flag. Cassie put it on and did a few modeling poses. She looked adorable. Jasper and I woofed our approval.

I desperately wanted to ask Cassie on a date. I hadn't been with a woman in over a year. I was lonely, but I also felt like I had an invisible force field around me, like in a science fiction movie. I was surrounded by the invisible force of my guilt and shame, with the added stink of desperation. I was never smooth with the ladies but it made me even weirder around them. I sat in the armchair near the window and petted Jasper while I watched Cassie. She methodically examined each article of clothing, priced it, then wrote the number on a pad.

"I haven't seen you in a while. Having too much fun?"

Cassie didn't know about my troubles and I wanted to keep it that way. "You know it," I said.

"I always like seeing what you bring in, you have a good eye. But this is a whole other level. Really fantastic."

Jasper raised his head from my knee and groped me with his paw. I went back to scratching him.

"Where are you living these days?"

"Long Island. About an hour out."

"Really? You don't strike me as the suburban type. Isn't it boring?"

"It is, but I'm kind of stuck there right now. Besides, sometimes I think boredom is the most interesting thing about the suburbs."

Cassie smiled.

"I think I know what you mean. I grew up in a small town and I hated it, but there was something character-building about it, I think. Around here you have a lot of hipsters who are into the coolest music, art, magazines, whatever, but it almost seems like a competition sometimes. Is that what you mean, about boring being good?"

"Maybe. I feel like I'm going crazy out there, but I'd probably feel that way anywhere."

Cassie stared into space. "'The problem with western man is that he does not know how to be content in an empty room'."

"Good one."

"It's not mine. Blaise Pascal said it."

"Well, next time you see Blaise, tell her I think she's a genius."

Cassie laughed. "It's not a she, it's a he. Pascal was a great mathematician and philosopher in the seventeenth century."

"Oh. Maybe you can add 'dumb' to the list of problems with the suburbs."

"You're not dumb. It was an obscure reference. I was being pretentious. See? Living here is rubbing off on me."

It took about half an hour in all. Cassie marked and priced the last few items, then punched the calculator and wrote down a figure. Then she frowned and added it up a second time.

"Okay, we're done. Can I give you a check? I don't have enough cash on hand."

"Can you split it? I'm pretty low until payday."

"Sure, not a problem." Cassie opened the register and counted out some bills. Then she removed the ledger from a drawer, wrote a check and tore it out. "Here you go. I'll just need you to sign a receipt for me, and I'll give you a copy as well."

"Of course." I gently lifted Jasper's head so I could get up from the chair. Cassie handed me the bills and check. I still felt vaguely like a criminal, which in a sense I was.

"I've only got a hundred and fifty in cash to spare," she said. "I hope that's all right."

"That's great."

"I priced the whole lot at twelve hundred, so your take is forty percent of that, or four hundred and eighty dollars. And if you find more stuff like this, we can work out a better deal. I'll give you fifty percent, since these are so scarce and desirable right now. Is that okay with you?"

"I was hoping to get twenty bucks for the cardigans and the surf shirt. This is totally unexpected."

"Oh, I forgot about those." She looked them over, priced them, opened the register and handed me another twenty. "Twenty it is. You're good at pricing this stuff. Sometimes I have to argue with people who think that they're getting ripped off. I tell them to bring their clothes to another shop, and they'll see that I'm the best game in town."

I stared at the check. Three hundred and thirty dollars and no cents. Plus one-seventy in cash. My best day ever. I signed the receipt with Daddy-O's pen and floated out.

I got back to the Olds and checked Daddy-O's card again for the address. I took the back way, down past the Navy Yard. The streets were quieter and that gave me time to think about how to spend my windfall.

Soon I was in the tangle of streets around Borough Hall. I lucked into a spot only a few blocks from Daddy-O's office. The pain in my neck and back had subsided into a constant drumbeat of misery, but I was getting used to it.

Pretty soon I realized what a mistake I had made. The people who work and live in downtown Brooklyn are not the same ones who cruise Bedford Avenue in

Williamsburg. I was no longer surrounded by groovy musicians, artists, and aspiring belly dancers. Between the courthouses and jail around there, I found myself in the thick of lawyers, cops, and the cool young blacks who worked and shopped up and down the Fulton Mall. I didn't just stick out like a sore thumb; I stuck out like a nation of sore thumbs, a world of sore thumbs. I was the visiting King of Sore Thumbnia.

I was openly gawked at; gaggles of young women shouted "Oh my God!" and had to hold each other up from laughing so hard when I passed; black shopkeepers and baggy teens alike called out comments that, how shall I say it, led me to suspect that I was not wearing what they considered to be the height of fashion. As I did my walk of shame I was followed by a trail of howls, laughter, and wails of disbelief. It was a social hazing like I had never experienced before. I kind of enjoyed it.

I made it to Adams Street and turned the corner. Something up the street caught my eye. It was a tight skirt, being carried with an amazingly sexual walk by a very attractive brunette. She was wearing knee-high patent leather boots, bright stockings, and a shiny blouse that looked fantastic. Her impressive physical assets and big hair were stacked and piled so far out and up that she wobbled through space like a continuously collapsing house of cards made out of nothing but the Queen Of Spades. It took a moment before I realized that the walk, the hair, and even the shiny boots were familiar to me. It was my ex-girlfriend, Devil Girl.

I fell back in a mad scramble. She had threatened to have me arrested and charged with harassment if I made contact with her, and I took her at her word. I knew she had moved to Brooklyn after we broke up, but it was such a big place that I had never even considered that we might run into each other some day.

I ducked behind a mailbox. To make myself look less suspicious I pulled the check out of my pocket, and the pen, and pretended to be doing some important business calculations. I peered over the mailbox and watched Devil Girl as she wobbled up the street. I thought I had it rough in the golf clothes; I couldn't imagine the comments she would have to endure on a daily basis, looking like that. She stopped in front of a building, and a moment later the door opened and a guy ran out and took her in his arms. They kissed deeply, for a good long time, and then the guy pulled away and I could see his face.

It was Daddy-O.

Where was I

Under threat of death or torture, or a lifetime in prison eating nothing but rats and living with a big bald dude who calls me Wifey, I could not tell you how I got back to Mumfrey that afternoon. I have no memory of the walk back to the car, the route I took, what the traffic was like, or how long the drive was. I don't know if you've ever had that experience, where you drive somewhere on autopilot and at the end of the trip you can't remember the trip itself. That's how I felt. I was in shock.

Devil Girl and Daddy-O. Officer Paul D'Addario and She Who Will Not Be Named. My probation officer and the girl I once loved. The future Mr. and Mrs. Daddy-O. Little Daddy-O Junior, running down the boardwalk at Long Beach. The names and scenarios kept rolling through my mind, over and over.

It wasn't just the shock of seeing them together, or the potential danger it presented for me, with my ex-girlfriend whispering in the ear of the guy who could make my life hell. It also confirmed my suspicions that our so-called justice system has everything to do with exerting power and punishment over the weak, and practically nothing to do with right or wrong. It didn't help my view of authority any.

But the real killer was that the moment I saw Devil Girl again I had realized with a sick feeling that I still wasn't over her. I had no control over the reaction she caused in me, how she sent my blood boiling and made my hands shake from the desire to tear every piece of tight, stylish clothing off her body. I am a man of strong passions and make no apologies for it, and if that offends you, I'm sorry.

I got back to Mumfrey late afternoon. I couldn't head back to the rooming-house. My head was killing me. I needed a drink. I couldn't afford a DUI but it was either that or jump in front of a train somewhere, and at that time of day most of them only ran once an hour.

I drove to my backup bar, the City View Tavern. It sits on one of the highest points in town; from the windows along the western wall you get a clear view of the distant jeweled crown of Manhattan, gray and immortal on the horizon. I ordered a beer and stared at the skyline. It looked so tiny and pretty. I wondered if I could ever go back there, live there, after what happened.

We had met at Cross County Community College, where I was studying audio engineering and sound production. Devil Girl was getting a degree in fashion. One day as I sat on a bench waiting for class to begin she complimented me on a jacket I was wearing, and we struck up a conversation. Pretty soon we were inseparable. When she graduated that spring I dropped out without getting my Associate's degree and we moved into the city together, into a small East Village apartment that we sublet from a friend of hers who was living in Spain for a few years.

It was harder finding work in the music business than I expected, especially without a degree, so I worked a series of menial jobs: bus boy, moving man, messenger. She found an entry-level position in the fashion business, which I thought was a fantastic break, but she decided she didn't like it after all. Which was a shame, because I think she could have been brilliant at it, but Devil Girl was also undisciplined. She lacked patience and had a ferocious temper.

We did what most young couples do in the city and started going out almost every night, watching bands and hanging out with an odd assortment of old and new friends, who were all beginning their adult lives too. A local band eventually asked me to help record and produce their demo; that should have been the beginning of my career, but shortly after I started going to rehearsals and then the recording studio with them, Devil Girl felt threatened and accused me of abandoning her. She began making comments about how if I couldn't appreciate her then she would find someone who did. This distressed me greatly, and in hindsight—and with Dr. K.'s help—I realize that she was intentionally knocking me off balance, wanting me to spin emotionally out of control, to feed her sick need for drama. But I was smitten; it wasn't just sexual to me, even though the sex was incredible. She had a genuinely fast mind and sharp wit, and I was truly in awe of her style. The band I was helping out broke up after a few weeks, but during that short period of time things had already changed between us. Devil Girl began going out alone some nights, claiming it was fair because, after all, I had spent those late nights in the studio, and I gave her all the freedom and space she said she wanted. Of course, it wasn't too long before she didn't come home one night, and the next day, after I had spent a sleepless night and was about to go to a dead-end job in a mail room, she announced tearfully that she had met someone and was moving in with him.

He was a singer-songwriter with a brilliant future, she said, and turned the knife by telling me that they had been fooling around on the sly for a few months, including in our studio apartment. Devil Girl moved out and the absentee landlord was surprisingly decent about it, and said I could stay for as long as I needed. That little kindness helped me over the initial grief, and since the rent was so low I figured I could stay there indefinitely, even on my crummy salary. I had saved some money that I wouldn't be using on college, and knew I could make it another year before I'd have real financial problems.

Devil Girl had only been gone a few weeks before the trouble started. Her new guy was doing lots of drugs, she said, hard stuff, and leaning on her for money. One night she called me, hysterical. She had refused to give her new boyfriend any more money and he had beaten her up and taken the cash from her purse. He said that if she was still in his apartment when he returned from scoring his drugs that he was going to kill her. I told her to call the police and get out of there fast, but Devil Girl was nearly incoherent with terror. I raced over to the building on the Bowery and she buzzed me up. As I got to the top of the stairs the boyfriend came barreling out of the apartment like he was coming after me, and I saw Devil Girl there by the door, sobbing, with two black eyes, and that's when I exploded.

Things get a bit fuzzy after that, but I remember my fists meeting his face, over and over and over, and then the next thing I knew, the future rock star was lying in a bloody pool at the bottom of the stairs, his limbs twisted in unnatural ways and his body broken in at least a dozen places. I remember looking down at my bloody hands, a sick feeling in my stomach, and Devil Girl screaming that I was crazy and a bastard and had no right to interfere.

It turned out that she had exaggerated quite a bit over the phone, both about the extent of her injuries and the danger she was in. Her two black eyes were nothing more than smeared mascara. The new boyfriend hadn't really hurt her at all, just pushed her once and stuck his thumb in her eye while she was attacking him. He had gone out to score more drugs, yes, but when the police took her statement she denied that she had said anything about him threatening to kill her. At first she even denied calling me, and made it seem like I had just appeared out of nowhere, but lucky for me the cops who responded to the scene got the truth out of her about that, so I not only had something to back up my version of events, but it hurt her credibility as well. That should have been the end of it, but the nightmare was just beginning.

The sensitive rock visionary was really the son of a wealthy and powerful man, some kind of ambassador or vice-consul or something, and he pulled strings or used political connections or something, because the full force of the law came crashing down on me. I was eventually charged with second degree assault, a class D felony, and was facing two to seven years behind bars.

My mom hasn't been very reliable about most things in my life—she's a pretty heavy drinker and therefore either preoccupied or depressed most of the time—but when the chips were down she outdid herself, and came through for me in a big way. She asked the Padre for his help, and her boss hooked us up with a decent lawyer who did the work for almost nothing. Fr. Pete even testified as a character witness in my defense. He spoke so beautifully about knowing me my whole life and watching me grow up, and how I was the most dependable altar boy he ever had—all of which was news to me, since we had spoken maybe a hundred words to each other my whole life—that he almost had the whole room in tears, including the judge and the prosecution. He said that if the judge would show mercy on me and release me with a suspended sentence, that he would guarantee me a job for the term of my probation.

Incredibly, everyone agreed. Even the victim's vindictive father, who I think at that point was less motivated by compassion than he was by the bad publicity he was getting as the father of a drug addict. We agreed to the deal and I was spared jail time. I couldn't believe it.

Some people said I got a raw deal, that if the roles had been reversed there was no way a rich kid would have gotten a similar sentence, but I didn't care. I was free, mostly, and I felt it was a pretty fair outcome considering what I had done.

My mom cried pretty much nonstop for a week after the trial was over, saying how happy she was. I was happy too, it could have been much worse, but it wasn't like I got off easy. In the span of a few months I had lost my girl, freedom, and future, stuck for three years in the one place I most want to get away from. The only funny part about it all is that I now work for a thrift shop and make extra money selling vintage clothes, so I guess you could say that I was the one who wound up in the fashion business.

I paid for the beer and got out of there. I hadn't eaten all day, so I stopped at the New Yangtze No. 1 Chinese Kitchen, better known as the Ew Skang Kee. The place is a grease pit, where the biggest seller is the fried chicken, French fries, and fried rice combo, a stomach-bombing steal at five bucks. For a dollar more you can get fried shrimp or fried fish, and you have your choice of beef, pork, or, for the health conscious, vegetable fried rice. I ordered the General Tso's chicken with fried rice combo, then walked down to the convenience store and picked up a six-pack of good beer. I got the provisions into the Olds and rumbled back to the rooming-house and went upstairs. That's when I discovered that the door had been kicked in, and my place had been ransacked.

The doorknob was loose, and the place where it clicks into the frame was cracked, but other than that, it was kind of hard to tell at first. My room always looks like it has been hit by a hurricane—maybe a sad, depressed hurricane, but still. The thin foam mattress from the cot was on the floor, exposing the cheap wood slats of the frame. The pillow had been pulled from the case and ripped open, its fluffy polyester guts hanging out of one side. The typewriter was on its back and my papers were scattered. The door to the fridge had been left open, causing the ice compartment to mostly defrost in the beastly heat, leaving a big puddle on the floor. I didn't have anything worth stealing, but whoever it was didn't know that, and had given the place a thorough going over.

I stood there, stunned, trying to take it all in, when I heard a gentle throat-clearing sound behind me. I spun around and saw Aku the Mystic looming in the doorway.

Aku lives down the hall from me, and he was the only one of my fellow roomers who I had spoken with. He's a wizard, and I don't mean a wizard at something else, like cooking or car engines. I mean he's a real, actual Wizard. He's about six foot six with long curly hair past his shoulders and a big full beard to match. His fingernails are about two inches long and always filthy. He's the freakiest guy I've ever seen, but he's actually really nice and doesn't drink or smoke or anything. He makes his living as a telephone psychic, which he can do right out of his room. Aku isn't a scammer; he's a true believer. He really studies all that New Age stuff and when you talk to him for a while you can start to believe it too.

Aku doesn't just call himself a wizard, he dresses like one too. He wears the most incredible costumes when he works, which he doesn't have to do since he works out of his room and nobody can see him. At the moment he was wearing a long, purple velvet robe that was covered with silver stars and moons.

"I'm sorry to have frightened you," Aku said in his deep, smooth voice. "But someone was in your room earlier."

"I can see."

"I thought it was you at first. I was on the phone with some clients, so I didn't think anything of it. Then the individual started making a great deal of noise and cursing, so I came out to investigate."

"What time was he here?"

"I'm not quite sure, but it wasn't too long ago. Maybe an hour. I had just emerged from a trance. I tend to lose track of time when I journey to the astral plane."

"What did he look like?"

"I didn't get a good look. When I emerge from the spirit realm it takes time for my eyes to adjust to the corporeal plane. Besides, the hallway was very dark. But I did speak briefly with him. He said you had something of his that he needed to get back. He was very intimidating. If I can remember anything else I'll let you know."

"That's all right. Thanks."

"Now if you'll excuse me, that's my phone. It's a client of mine. She's trying to determine the best time of the year to schedule plastic surgery, based on the transits of Mercury and Saturn."

"I don't hear anything."

We both paused for about five seconds. Then the phone in Aku's room started to ring. I stared at him.

"Damn, you're good."

"Thank you." He gave a little bow and smiled. "But she always calls exactly at this time. She's very prompt."

Aku filtered out and went back to his room. For a big guy he didn't make any noise. I wondered if he was naturally graceful or if his robe acted as a kind of muffler. I closed the broken door as best I could and started putting the room back together.

Yay

My bed sheet was still hanging from the curtain rod, where it had been since my shower that morning. I used it to dry the puddle of defrosted ice on the floor and it picked up a depressing amount of filth. I hung it back up to dry, but it was ruined. I put the drawers back into the dresser, gathered my scattered papers, and put the cot back the way it belonged. Then I sat on the floor and tried to eat. The food was cold and the beer was warm.

I was tired and hung-over the next morning. I didn't fall asleep until after two, after I had blocked the door by leaning the desk chair under the knob. It was after ten when I woke up. The humidity had subsided during the night and there was even a bit of a breeze blowing, so I actually felt pretty good for a change. I still had a lot of stiffness in my neck, and my head was sore to the touch, but at least my physical injuries were healing. Emotionally, I wasn't doing so well. I felt violated, angry, and afraid; every time I heard a noise in the hallway, I jumped. Luckily I had errands to do that would get me out of my room for most of the day.

No more golf outfits for me. I took the money I had made from Cassie out of the golf pants and got back into my smelly and stiff work clothes from the day before and drove down to the convenience store. I got two large coffees, ham and egg on a roll and a fat square of coffee cake, then drove to the town dock and ate breakfast while making a list of things I needed.

The first stop was the gas station, where I filled up the Olds. Then I went to my bank and deposited the check using the drive-through machine, and from there to the big shopping mall a few miles south of town. An hour later I came out carrying several bags, filled with new work pants, tube socks, boxer briefs, and several pocket T-shirts. I also had new towels and sheets, and a free spritz of cologne that one of the ladies in a department store was nice enough to offer me. I had spent over a hundred dollars, which was more than I had spent on myself for as long as I could remember. I spent the next couple of hours putting on the new sheets, laying out the pants and T-shirts in different combinations, then took a long, hot shower with my new bath towel close at hand. By the time I was done I had just enough time to get dressed and over to St. Boniface for the Tortura wedding.

As I played with the damaged doorknob, trying to get it to lock properly, I heard Aku's gentle cough behind me.

"Excuse me, Bert, but I just remembered something else about the man who was in your room yesterday. He spoke with a southern accent. I don't know if it helps, but I thought I should mention it."

"That does help, thanks."

Aku bowed and faded into the wood paneling.

Under normal circumstances I would have called Daddy-O and reported what happened and asked his advice, but these weren't normal circumstances. If I called him now it would be an ugly conversation. I started shaking just thinking about it. And it seemed too crazy and complicated to explain to Dr. K., and besides, it wasn't the type of situation that I could solve just by doing The Calisthenics of Love or whatever. I was on my own.

St. Boniface was a zoo. A long line of cars stretched down the street in both directions, and several traffic cops kept the peace. Cruisers with their lights going, flares burning. Quite a scene. I took the back way, which allowed me to avoid the crunch but meant I had to go the wrong way at one point, up a small one-way street that led into the rear of the church parking lot. I got my usual spot behind Bonnie's Bag, on an overgrown little patch of broken concrete and weeds. I was early, but I wanted to get a peek at the beautiful young lady who had smiled at me.

I went into the sacristy. The Padre was putting on the final parts of his costume, getting ready for the show. He seemed happy to see me, which was not an expression people usually got when I walked into a room.

"Thank goodness you're here. You must have heard my prayers. We have a problem. Brian Corrigan was supposed to be my other server today, but his mother called and said he's broken his arm. I was wondering if you would fill in for him?"

"Me?"

"You'll have Jimmy here to guide you."

A freckled little squirt, who looked about ten years old, raised his hand and smiled weakly.

"Hi."

"'Sup."

I hadn't been an altar boy since the eighth grade, and even then I wasn't a very good one. The first mass I served, I dropped the glass cruets that held the wine and water and they smashed on the marble floor in front of the altar. My mom bought the church a new set, but I was forever marked as the Cruet Smasher. It was all downhill from there.

"I don't know, Father—"

The Padre gave me a look of such hopeful innocence, such kindness, that I couldn't refuse. I exhaled with a defeated shrug.

"Of course, I'll be glad to do it."

"Wonderful. There's a spare cassock and surplice in the cabinet that might fit. If not then we'll have to improvise. We've only got a couple of minutes before the prelude."

I'll spare you the gruesome details. I assume you've been to at least a few weddings, maybe even your own.

This was just like any other, except with a little more hair product and shiny fabrics, even by Long Island standards. The only memorable part, for me anyway, was when the bridesmaids came down the aisle and I saw her again. Me and the kid they called Jimmy were in our seats by the side of the altar, mostly hidden from view. She was more beautiful than I remembered. She took her seat in the front row with the other bridesmaids and I leaned over to see her better. I leaned over so far that the chair I was on tipped over. I had to put out both my arms and slam my foot on the marble floor to keep from landing on my face, causing a big *slap* sound that echoed around the church. The next time I peeked around the corner I saw the little Tortura girl looking at me, grinning ear to ear.

I really don't remember anything after that, except that I stole glances at her every chance I got. I followed Jimmy's lead and didn't break any glassware or take any more falls. When it was time for communion I stood on the side of the aisle with the bridesmaids. My little angel kept herself in character and took the host in her mouth with piety and grace. She had beautiful teeth.

When mass was over I loitered around the exit hoping to catch a glimpse of her, but the crowds were too thick, both in number and girth. I couldn't see her through the forest of tuxedos and taffeta, chins and belly fat, so I went back into the sacristy and pulled off the robes. Scotty Murrow, the church organist at St. Boniface, bounced into the room. He's small and trim, with neatly parted hair and a little mustache, and he adds a bit of show business attitude to the church that I like.

"Well, Bert, what a surprise. You certainly look nice in a dress."

"Thanks. You played very well today."

"You think so? I'm worried that it went over their heads. Philistines. Do you know what the bride and groom asked me to play as a wedding march? A song called 'Wonderful Tonight.' Do you know it?"

"Yeah, it's by Eric Clapton."

"Horrible song, absolutely atrocious."

"Amen."

"I told them it would be a better choice for the reception, and that I wouldn't be able to learn any new material on such short notice. Just made up any excuse I could. Luckily they didn't insist, and let me pick the music."

"Good for you."

"Indeed. What are you doing after this?"

"Cleaning up. Why?"

"How would you like to earn a few bucks?"

"What do I have to do?"

"I've been hired to play keyboards at the reception. Just background music, in the house. I could use a page turner." He winked at me.

"A what?"

"You know, someone to turn the pages of the sheet music while I play." He winked again. "I could pay you." Wink. Wink.

"Thanks," I said, feeling creeped out, "but I don't think so. That's not my scene." I winked back at him. Scotty sighed.

"Lord, you're dense. I'm not hitting on you, stupid. I thought you would like to turn pages, quote-unquote, so you could have a chance to talk to that cute maid of honor you kept staring at through the service."

"Was I that obvious?"

"I could see you gawking at her all the way from the organ loft. And my back was turned."

"Thanks anyway, but I think I'll pass."

Scotty shrugged. "Suit yourself."

One of the guests came up to Scotty and thanked him, and I slipped away through the crowds and went back across the parking lot. Sneaking into a wedding reception to stalk a girl I didn't know wasn't exactly my idea of a good time. Especially not with the Torturas, who were notorious as Mumfrey's resident mafia family.

I normally don't clean the church, but Manny, the full-time janitor who lives over the thrift shop, was on a trip back to Mexico to visit his ailing father. He would be gone for a few weeks, and the Padre had asked me to fill in as necessary. I went out to the Olds to get my work gloves. I noticed a piece of paper under the one of the wipers. I reached around and pulled it out. It had been torn from a notebook, and the writing was done in block lettering:

YORE DEAD FAGIT

was all it said.

My legs felt weak. I scanned the parking lot, looking for any sign of the van. It was so crowded that I didn't think he would try anything there, but I was still terrified. He had found my home, my place of work. Nowhere felt safe right then, except maybe the home of Mumfrey's most notorious mafia family.

As I ran back to the church, I saw my angel standing there, just outside the door, smiling. She was holding something in her hands. She started to say something. I blew past her without a word and ran through the church and out the front doors. Scotty was parked in the small strip along the side that's reserved for employees, about to drive off. I ran to his car and banged on the window. He lowered it, looking at me like I was crazy.

"Bert?! What is it, what's wrong?"

"On second thought," I gasped, trying to catch my breath, "I would love to be your page turner."

"Um, okay. The reception doesn't start for a couple of hours; they're doing the photos first. Do you want me to give you a ride, or would you rather run there?"

I wheezed. "Can you come by here so I can follow you over?"

"I'll return at six. In the meantime, try not to have a heart attack, okay? It's only a gig."

Great

The Tortura compound was in the most remote and exclusive section of Pondington. Even in Pondington there were better and worse neighborhoods. The people with ten acres looked down on the people with five; the people with six bedrooms envied the people who had twelve. I doubted that the Torturas envied anyone. They had supposedly made their money in carting and hauling, construction and real estate—everything from fast food joints to car washes to office parks—but the word around town was that old man Tortura had earned his money the old-fashioned way, killing people.

If I didn't know better, the first time I saw their house I would have thought that Mr. Tortura was some kind of insane cupcake mogul. The place was surrounded by giant white stucco walls, topped with blue and pink marble bowling balls with halogen spotlights glowing from within, lighting the trees around the perimeter in different colors. The effect from the street was of a monstrous, computer-generated birthday cake, an offering made to some race of sweet-toothed aliens who might someday return.

Big guys waved lighted poles, directing people where to park along the side of the road. Scotty pulled up to the first guy and talked to him. I saw him motion to my car, and the big guy looked at me, then talked into a walkie-talkie. The gate swung open. Scotty pulled in, and I followed behind. The guy with the walkie-talkie said "nice car" as I drove by. I never get tired of hearing that.

The driveway went up a hill, long and winding, and ended in a gravel circle around a huge marble fountain, with a giant statue of some muscular guy spouting water from his mouth. We found spaces among the stretch SUVs, military-grade Cadillacs, and armored Lincolns that were parked all over. The place looked like some half-assed Saudi Arabian used car dealership. The Olds is a tank, but next to these monsters it looked like a tricycle. Scotty's compact looked like a hood ornament.

I grabbed the amplifier. Scotty took the keyboard and another bag and we walked in. The gilt doors were as big as twin bank vaults; two beefy white-gloved attendants opened them for us. Scotty turned to me.

"I could get used to living like this."

"You and me both."

Not even the gaudiness of the exterior had prepared me for what was inside. It looked like a group of Las Vegas showgirls had hijacked an armored car and crashed into Liberace's grave. It was all smooth, reflective surfaces: white marble, pink marble, blue marble, red marble; chrome and glass, silver and gold. There were polished, gleaming surfaces everywhere, including a generous helping of floor-to-ceiling mirrors, giving the feel of a funhouse in a mausoleum. There was no wood or fabric anywhere that I could see. I assumed this obsession with nonporous and reflective surfaces was to make it easier for the Torturas and their associates to clean up the blood when they knocked off a stool pigeon, or to make it harder for some turncoat *consigliere* to sneak up on the old man and garrote him with a piece of steel spaghetti.

Scotty and I were directed by another security goon to a big, carpeted lounge on the lower level. We put the equipment down in a corner and Scotty started to set up.

"Can I do anything?"

"Could you bring me a Diet Coke? We'll be starting in fifteen minutes or so."

I went through the sliding doors and onto one of many patios. The yard was terraced, cut with a series of platforms down to the main wedding area below. Deep stone steps, as wide as gymnasium bleachers, went down to another basketball court-sized patio, and beyond that was an enormous circus tent, strung with glittering white lights. Tables went around the edge of the dance floor, each crammed with crystal and linen and silver. A full band, with horns and violins and a harp and everything, was set up on the far side of the tent, playing a peppy number while the bandleader crooned in Italian. An army of waiters in formal attire scurried around with silver trays of food.

There was a commotion from the back of the house on a level above me, screams and cheering accompanied by the burst of flashbulbs. The bride and groom waddled onto the upper patio to a round of applause. Mr. Tortura was beaming and shaking hands and hugging people, while a film crew captured every priceless moment. There was much yelling and grabbing of shoulders, kissing and sobbing. Finally I saw my little angel. She looked so happy and beautiful that I couldn't help but smile. She glanced down, in my direction. Like an idiot I grinned at her and waved. Her smile dropped and she walked away. I slunk off to get the Cokes.

I did all right, considering I can't read music. Scotty would nod when it was time for me to turn the page. I only messed up a couple of times, going ahead two pages instead of one, then having to scramble back before he got lost. Then I relaxed and got into a rhythm.

The lounge was a large room with plenty of comfortable seating and soft lighting. Guests wandered in and out, sat and talked for a while, taking a break from the rest of the party. Scotty could really tinkle the ivories. He played different styles, and mixed them up in interesting ways. The guests liked it too: Scotty's tip jar filled up quickly. A few drunks came up and stuffed twenties into it. It was a very pleasant scene.

After an hour, Scotty turned off the keyboard and stood up, just as a tipsy guest was asking if he knew any songs by Keesha or Meesha or something. Scotty declined politely, saying that he would be right back, and the disappointed young lady wobbled away on her heels.

"Break time," he said. "We get fifteen minutes for each hour we work. It's in the contract. Let's go out and get something to eat. I bet they have marvelous food here."

The sky overhead had turned to a deep indigo; stars were beginning to pop out of the velvety darkness. Things were in full swing. Wine and champagne were flowing, there was loud talk and happy faces everywhere. The orchestra was chugging along and the old ladies were ruling the dance floor, clapping and dipping, pointing the stubby toes of their swollen feet this way and that, holding their hips with one hand and swirling the other around their heads as they spun with abandon. There was something about the old people dancing that was strangely beautiful to me, as if they were laughing at life for not being able to get them down.

The bride and groom, each surrounded by a small coterie of attendants, were seated at the main table, watching the fun. I saw something being passed around the table. It was a pink satin bag. Each person who got the bag put something in it, either a card or an envelope. Scotty pointed it out to me.

"Look at that," he whispered, "they really do pass around a money bag, just like in *The Godfather*."

"Marone."

We went over to one of the buffet tables. It was an incredible spread. A line of stiffs in white jackets loaded my plate with pasta, shrimp, and salad. We found an empty table on the edge of the party, away from the others. It was a good time to see if Scotty knew anything about Corky Healey, since he seemed so connected.

"Oh, that poor man," he said, alternating between bites of lasagna and mussels, "and what a lovely funeral. I hope they catch whoever did it."

"You think it might be foul play?"

Scotty dabbed the cloth napkin at his mouth, and held up a finger while he finished chewing and swallowed. "You can't tell anyone I told you this; I'll deny I said it."

I pulled an invisible zipper across my lips. "Omerta."

"I heard that he was involved in some shady business deals that went bad, involving..." Scotty twirled his finger around.

"Helicopters?"

"Um, no."

"The Torturas?"

Scotty touched his nose. "Ding ding! And to think, some people say you're slow."

"What kind of deals?"

He lifted a stalk of grilled asparagus and held it up, like an orchestra conductor about to start.

"I don't know. Something about real estate, I think." He shrugged. "I hear lots of things through the church, and by playing gigs like this. Sometimes the rumors are true, sometimes they're just idle gossip, a chance to settle old scores."

"Mrs. Healey told me that one of his golf clubs is missing."

"Really? Interesting. That's a new one. Another theory I heard was that his son had been cut out of the old man's will, and that he went out on the course that morning and had a fight with his father and that's when it happened. More of an accident than a murder, but still a cover-up." Scotty snapped off the head of the asparagus with his teeth. "Why are you so interested in all of this?"

"Mrs. Healey is offering a reward for the return of his missing golf club."

"Ah." Scotty thought this over as we ate in silence. I wasn't sure about Dale being involved; I doubted he would have been so forthcoming about the details, or so calm. It seemed more plausible to me that the Torturas had something to do with it. I hoped not, because I had a serious crush on one of them and I was eating their food.

Screw it. I popped another shrimp into my mouth.

"Aren't you a little old to be an altar boy?"

I turned around, startled. The tail of the shrimp was sticking out of my mouth, dripping butter down my chin. It was my angel. She had changed out of the taffeta dress and was wearing tight white pants, a silvery-blue blouse, and beautiful strap sandals. She had let her hair down, and it was dark brown and silky and cascaded past her shoulders. She was in a whole different class from what I was used to. Devil Girl looked like a streetwalker compared to her. She was giving me the once-over, arms folded, tapping her tiny foot on the grass in that sexy sandal.

Scotty looked at his watch and stood up. "My, how time flies. Break's over. You stay and relax, Bert, I can handle it for a while."

He hustled off, leaving me there. I gulped the shrimp down and wiped butter off my chin. "Excuse me?"

"I said, aren't you a little old to be an altar boy?"

"I don't know. Aren't you a little old to be a bridesmaid?"

"Not at all. I'm only twenty-two."

I thought of the first snappy comeback I could. "Ah," I said. "Right."

"I tried giving this to you before." She held out her hand. There was an envelope in it. I took the envelope and peeked inside. I saw some bills.

"What's this?"

"For serving the mass. We tip everybody involved; it's bad luck not to. You almost jinxed it, the way you blew me off at the church."

"I didn't mean to. It was kind of important."

"I see." She didn't say any more. She stood there, arms folded, staring at me. Her face went from hard to a kind of playful smile.

"You don't remember me, do you?"

"Of course I do. I saw you at the church. I'm sorry I was so rude."

"Not that. We've met before, don't you remember?"

"I can't imagine how I could forget, but I'm sorry, I don't."

"We took English together junior year, with Mr. Bocarde. Well, you were a junior but I was actually a grade behind you. I got placed into it as an honors course."

High school seemed like a lifetime ago, and what little I remembered about those days I had already forgotten.

"Oh yeah," I said vaguely. "Sure, I remember."

She shook her head. "You are the world's worst liar, Bert." She extended her hand and I took it. It was a small hand, with incredibly delicate fingers, warm and soft and strong. I didn't want to let it go. "I'm Ariabella Tortura. Aria."

"Bert Shambles."

"Yes, I know."

"Look, I'm really sorry. I don't know why I don't remember you; it's crazy. You're completely unforgettable."

She smiled. "Not back then. I was very plain and chubby, and had glasses, braces, and crazy hair. I pretty much kept to myself. I was too shy to talk to anybody."

"Well, if it's any consolation, I have gotten my payback. You're as beautiful as a model or a movie star, so now you get to laugh at jerks like me who didn't pay any attention to you back in high school."

"Speaking of jerks like you, what are you doing here?"

"Scotty asked me to be his page turner. I've got to get back to him, actually."

"I thought he just said he could handle it."

"Yes. But I'm not sure that I can."

"You're funny. Go ahead and turn your pages, I'll check in on you later. Just be careful not to get a paper cut."

I went inside and picked up where I left off. Scotty saw my big goofy grin and spoke under his breath. "Guess it went well?"

"Pretty good."

After a while Aria came into the lounge, and curled up in a corner of the big sectional sofa, watching us. Whenever I looked over at her and our eyes met she would give me a big smile, but sometimes when I stole a glance and she wasn't paying attention she had a more sad, thoughtful expression on her face. Finally Scotty leaned over and whispered that he could handle things for a while; he was going to do some improvisation. I went over to the couch and sat next to Aria.

"Well done. You have quite a talent."

"It's all in the wrist."

"If I stay here I'm going to fall asleep. Do you want to get outside for a bit? I was thinking of walking down to the beach."

It was an offer I couldn't refuse. I got up and followed her. I motioned to Scotty, he nodded, and then started a jazzy version of "Wonderful Tonight." I gave him the finger behind my back.

Mama mia

We walked along the edge of the property, away from the party, across a huge expanse of sloping lawn that was dotted with dogwoods and willows, birch and beech trees. I knew which were which because of a landscaping job I had one summer.

Aria was enjoying the night air, sometimes stopping and closing her eyes, taking deep breaths and occasionally looking at the sky.

"These family weddings are murder. All these relatives come out of the woodwork, plus all my father's associates. It's exhausting."

"It all seems pretty nice."

Aria sighed. "Not for me. I'd do anything to get out of here. This isn't who I am at all."

The grounds leveled off and then sloped back up to a wooded area. I turned and saw the faint lights of the party, the dreamy echo of the orchestra and the forbidding silhouette of the house behind it, glowing from within. I wondered what the electric bills were like.

"So what do you do? I mean, besides altar-boying and turning pages."

"I work part-time at the St. Boniface thrift shop, and make extra money doing odd jobs when I can."

"Didn't I hear that you got into some kind of trouble?"

"Yes. I'm on probation for three years."

"I'm so sorry. Can I ask what you got in trouble for?"

"My ex-girlfriend—" I stopped. No. I couldn't say it that way any more. I took a deep breath. "I lost my temper and I hurt someone really bad. I was charged with aggravated assault."

A cloud passed over her face. "You mean, you assaulted your ex-girlfriend?"

"No, not her. The jerk who was beating up on her. Or who I *thought* was beating up on her. I don't know. Maybe I imagined it all and only heard what I wanted to hear."

Aria looked at me with that same calm, confident sweetness. Then she did something that I wasn't expecting. She reached out and put her hand on my upper arm and rubbed it. It was unconscious and natural, a gentle and soothing gesture of simple human tenderness, but it went off like a bomb inside me.

"My family aren't exactly saints," she said softly. "My brothers have been in all kinds of trouble. And my sister—" Aria grunted. "My sister is—I can't even talk about her; it would be a sin to say bad things about her on her wedding day."

"So you're not totally disgusted with me?"

She smiled. "Not totally."

I followed her through the woods along a narrow dirt path, blindly at first and then with more confidence as my eyes adjusted. The trees were thick so it was very dark. My only guide was Aria's white pants, which meant that I could look at her rear end without feeling guilty. She had a magnificent specimen: small, round, and firm, each step flexing with the same playful confidence as her smile. Yes, her butt was smiling at me. And at the top, just over the waist of the pants, I thought I could make out the telltale fabric triangle of a thong.

Marone.

Maybe I was a pig, but a man's eyes have to eat just the same as his stomach. I wanted my eyes to get filled up on Aria's beautiful body to get me through the long, lonely days ahead. I had no illusions about it: girls like Aria didn't go out with guys like Bert Shambles, and if you think they do then you read too many romance books or watch the wrong kind of TV shows. Only the nature programs show how it really works, how only the dominant male gets to breed. And to be dominant as a human animal you needed money, connections, or power. At the very least, you had to have a chance of attaining at least one of the three, and I didn't see any of them in my future.

The path opened out onto a wooden platform on top of a cliff, with a staircase zig-zagging down to the sand far below. We were high above Mumfrey Bay. I looked out at the inky blackness of the water, the tips of the gentle waves glinting in the moonlight. Across the bay, I could see the twinkling lights of other compounds like this one, palaces of success, the homes of dominant men. I was so tired of my crappy life. I had half a mind to swim out into that black water and disappear for good.

I felt something soft slip into my hand. I looked over. It was Aria. She smiled up at me.

"Everything okay? You look upset."

"I'm okay," I said. "Thanks."

"Ready to see the beach?"

"Sure."

Her hand slipped out of mine like a dream and she floated down the staircase.

We sat on an old, broken-down sea wall. To our left was a dock, extending far out into the bay. A nice-looking motorboat was tied up, white and sleek.

"That yours?"

Aria squinted at it. "Nope. It looks like Mr. Shanley's. He lives just down the beach. A few of us share this dock."

"So why wasn't it you?"

"Why wasn't it me what?"

"Up there getting married today."

Aria laughed. "Don't depress me. Some day, maybe. I want it to be for real, for a good reason."

"Your sister's not doing it for a good reason?"

"She doesn't love him. It's just money and property she's after."

"What kind of guy do you want to marry?"

"Wow, this conversation is moving quickly." I started to stammer an apology and she punched my arm. "I'm just messing with you. God, you're easy. You must really like me."

Aria put her hand on my thigh. It was like when she rubbed my arm, warm without being aggressive or sexual. I have no problem taking control when I'm with a woman, but I prefer if she makes the first move and signals her interest in some way. That's how they do it on the nature programs, anyway.

What the hell. I had to try something. I closed my eyes and leaned in for the kill. Her hand came up to my face and held me back. I opened my eyes and looked through her fingers.

"What happened?"

"Shh! Someone's coming."

Two figures were walking down to the beach. She swung her legs to the other side of the sea wall and dropped down. I followed her and we crouched behind the crumbling cement wall, huddled together among the fallen rubble and debris.

"It might be someone in my family," she said softly. "They're all so nosy and gossipy. I don't want to see anyone right now."

As we crouched together I could smell her hair and perfume, hear her breathing, her warm body pressed against mine. She steadied herself by holding onto my thigh again, only more firmly this time. I noticed she was shivering slightly, or at least I thought she was, so I put my arm around her shoulders. She snuggled closer.

We heard the engine of the yacht start up, then we peeked over the wall. One figure was at the wheel, while the other guy untied the ropes. I couldn't see who was driving but I recognized the other guy. It was Carrot Top. I felt sick to my stomach. My injured neck spasmed at the sight of him.

In a moment the yacht had backed up and was puttering slowly across the bay. Aria stood up.

"It was only Mr. Shanley. He's probably on his way home. I don't know who the other guy was, though."

"Who?"

"Bill Shanley. He's a big investment guy."

"I met him the other day. Sort of. He slammed a door in my face."

"That sounds like Bill. He can be very unpleasant. But I guess he's really good at what he does, because he's got more money than God." She brushed the sand off her pants. "I guess we should be heading back."

I turned away for a moment as I adjusted my pants. Aria went up on her toes, reached around and pulled my head down. She kissed me on the mouth, quickly but with feeling.

"Thank you for being such a gentleman," she said softly.

Being a gentleman had nothing to do with it. I helped her over the wall, then climbed over and dropped to the sand.

We were halfway back across the property when we heard the sound. It sounded like an alarm at first, a long, wailing sound like an air raid siren.

"That's my sister," Aria said. "I know her cry anywhere. Come on!"

We ran back to the house. The party was in a commotion. The band had stopped playing, old ladies were sobbing, and the men were standing in small groups, talking excitedly to each other. Aria ran over to her sister, and I decided to find out what was going on from Scotty. He was in the lounge, packing up.

"There you are," he said. "You missed all the excitement."

"What happened? Did the bride and groom have a fight or something?"

"No, they have a whole lifetime for that. Somebody stole the bag."

"You mean the bride?"

"No, the wedding purse, with all the money."

"Who would be crazy enough to do such a thing, with all the muscle around here?"

Scotty shrugged. "The party is over, obviously. We should get out of here." He packed the cords and sheet music into a backpack, and I got the amplifier again. "How was your time with Aria? Did you two get acquainted?"

"It was going great until now."

A big guy stalked into the lounge and pointed to Scotty and me.

"You two. Outside. Now."

We went out to the patio. There were a couple of other tough guys there, hyped up and itching for a fight. One of them stepped forward.

"Who are you two? What are you doing here, and where have you been for the last hour?"

Scotty went first. "I've been playing the keyboard in there. And this is my assistant."

"That's right," one of the other big guys said. "You played the organ at the wedding." He turned his attention to me. "And you were helping Tinkerbell here the whole time?"

"Yes," I stammered.

"That's bull." It was one of the other goons. "I saw him walking up from the back of the property just now." The main goon came up to my chest and looked down at me, his nostrils flaring.

"Izzat true? You out taking a little walk?"

"Yes."

"So you just lied to me."

"No. I mean, I can explain. I was helping, but then Scotty said I could take a break, and I went down to the beach."

"So when you was supposed to be in there you just decided to take a little walk around our property without permission? You expect us to believe that?"

I shook my head. I couldn't rat Aria out, not after she had told me about how overbearing and controlling her family was. Now I understood what she meant.

"Look, I didn't steal anything," I said. "I don't know anything about it."

"Maybe we can help you remember."

The goons moved in. The big guy grabbed me by the collar of my new Sears work shirt. I felt my knees going weak again. I covered my face with my hands and tried to remember how to say a prayer.

"Stop it!"

It was Aria. She slapped the big guy's hand off me and stood between us, glaring up at him. "Bert was with me the whole time."

The big goon stepped back. "What are you sayin'?"

"I'm telling you what happened," she snapped. "I took a walk with Bert, and we went down to the beach. What the hell business is it of yours?"

The big guy put up his hands in surrender. "Okay, sis, cool it." He shook his head. "Now I know why mom and dad worry about you so much." This earned the big guy a sharp slap on his ear, which made him cringe. "Ow, stop it! I'm sorry, all right?"

"No, it's not all right! This isn't something you can solve by beating up my friends!"

"Actually, beating up people has always worked pretty good," one of the other goons said.

"Shut up, Vito." The one she called Vito fell silent. Aria turned to me.

"Bert, please forgive my brothers. We're all obviously very upset about what has happened."

"Thank you," I said. "I'm very sorry about your sister, and I swear I had nothing to do with it."

"I know. But it's probably better if you leave now. Things are going to be bad around here for a while."

Scotty raised his hand. His voice dripped with sarcasm. "Can Tinkerbell please be excused too?"

I helped Scotty get his gear loaded back into his car. We didn't say much. Scotty slammed the trunk of his little hatchback.

"Thanks for your help, Bert. Oh, and here—" He reached into his pocket and handed me a small wad of bills.

"What's this?"

"Your cut from the tip jar, plus a little something extra, for your help. I know it didn't work out well, but I really appreciate it."

I tried handing it back. "I can't take this. I didn't do anything."

"You helped a lot, actually. Get home safe."

I felt sad as I walked back to the Olds. It could have been a magical night, if not for Carrot Top, the stolen money, and her stupid brothers. I didn't know what the hell was going on and I was too tired and depressed to think about it. I had been so close to kissing her.

There was a line of cars waiting to leave the grounds, merging with the street traffic. Scotty was a couple of cars ahead of me, with a white Mercedes and stretch limo between us. It was moving very slowly. I heard a guard tell the driver ahead of me that all the cars were being checked on the way out. Every time a car went through the gate there was another long wait. I turned on the radio to catch the news. When I finally got to the gate of the property, near the road, I could see the roadblock up ahead. Several big guys with flashlights were stopping each car, questioning the drivers, leaning into the windows, asking questions, and grilling all the other occupants. Once in a while a hood would be popped or one of the guys would get down on his back and look under the carriage. In a way it made me feel better. At least it wasn't only me getting the third degree.

I remembered a pack of cigarettes that I had bought a few weeks earlier. I don't smoke often but I really needed one right then. I fished the pack out of the glove compartment, got a butt, and pushed in the car's old metal lighter. The limo was waved through and the guards motioned for me to move ahead. The lighter popped out. I tried lighting the cigarette but the guard yelled at me to move and it startled me. I misjudged the distance and nearly clipped a convertible BMW by the side of the road. As I grabbed the wheel with both hands the red-hot lighter fell between my legs. I missed the BMW, cursed, and the Olds lurched forward. I almost ran into one of the guards but slammed on the brakes just in time. He cursed and said "Whoa whoa whoa!" I reached under the seat, trying to find the lighter before it set the whole damn car on fire. My hand touched something smooth. I pulled it up. It was a very pink, very satin, and very stolen wedding purse. It was empty.

The guard was almost at the car. He did not look happy. He was yelling something I couldn't understand. I looked at him helplessly, then saw that the way ahead was clear. The Olds spat gravel and dust, and the guards screamed and jumped out of the way as I floored it out of there.

Yeah

It wasn't my finest moment. I could have just pulled over, shown them the bag, and explained how I had found it under my seat. I'm sure they would have believed me. We would have laughed about it and then they would have invited me in for cake and coffee. Sure.

No, for once I would be smart, and do what every politician, CEO, or other pillar of society does and deny everything. I'd throw the damn satchel out the window, burn it, chop it up and bury it somewhere. I picked up a twelve-pack and finally dozed off in the early morning hours, watching a documentary about Canadian Geese.

I stayed in bed until noon, thinking about what to do, until hunger made me get up. I decided that I would tell Aria the truth, explain what happened, and hope she believed me. A good lunch somewhere might give me some inspiration, as I tried to figure out how to tell her. Scotty had given me fifty bucks for hardly doing anything, and there was another fifty in the envelope that Aria had given me. I kept getting chased, beaten up, and framed, but at least I was making some money for once.

The pink wedding satchel was on the floor. I would deal with it when I got back. It looked guilty just lying there like that, so I stuffed it into the bottom drawer of the dresser. I put the money in my wallet and started looking for my keys.

There was a gentle knock on the door. I walked over and pressed my ear against it. "Who's there?" I growled.

"Bert, is that you?"

It was Aria. I couldn't believe it. Was it a trap? I looked back at the dresser to make sure the drawer was closed. It was. I opened the door. She was wearing dark blue designer jeans with a different pair of sandals, and a white top with thin shoulder straps. Her skin was a color I can only describe as milky golden brown. Her presence made me suddenly aware of how ugly, depressed, and horrible my living situation was. Daddy-O was right to criticize me. I blocked her view of the room.

"How did you find me?"

"I have my ways." She saw the look on my face. "You're in the phone book, silly. I was going to call, then decided to swing by after church and see if you were home. I hope you don't mind."

"I was just on my way out to lunch. Why don't you join me?"

Her eyes brightened. "I'd love to! I just got out of mass. I haven't eaten yet today. I'm starving."

I got my keys from the desk. Aria stepped into the room and looked around.

"I like your place."

"Very funny."

"I'm serious. I admire a man who lives simply. Jesus lived without possessions, you know."

"Yeah, and look what happened to him."

Aria went over to the cot and sat gently on the edge of the mattress. "Before we go to lunch, can we talk for a minute?"

"Of course." I closed the door and took the chair.

"I heard you drove off in quite a hurry last night."

"A lighter dropped between my legs. I lost control, then I just kept going. I'm sorry."

She seemed relieved. "Why doesn't that surprise me? It did seem suspicious, but I figured there was an explanation. I also figured that after the hard time my brothers gave you,

I couldn't blame you for wanting to get away as soon as possible."

"True."

"I also wanted to talk to you about the missing money."

"Funny you should mention that. I wanted to talk to you about that too. But could we talk about it over lunch? I'm going to pass out if I don't eat soon. I'll drive."

I knew that I should just give her the purse but I was afraid that she would run right home and explain everything to her family. And I wanted to have as much time with her as I could, maybe even get a date out of it.

Aria smiled. "Sure. That sounds really nice."

There was a gentle knock on the door. "That's probably Aku," I said. I got up to open the door. Aria had moved the curtain and was looking out the window.

"Which car is yours? Is it the white van?"

I processed this too late. As soon as I turned the knob, the door swung hard and slammed into me, knocking me flat on my back. Aria screamed as a body piled on top of me.

Knees dug into my chest and something cold and hard began to squeeze my throat. The horrible, freckled face of Carrot Top snarled down at me. He was deranged, mad, insane, slobbering and baring his teeth, growling like a dog. He knelt on my chest and whatever cold and hard thing he had against my neck was choking me. I couldn't breathe. I felt the pressure in my head building, hot and suffocating. I craned my eyes to the right. Aria had pulled her legs up onto the cot to avoid our falling bodies. She was moving her mouth but I couldn't hear what she was saying. I could just make out the end of what was causing the pressure against my neck: it was a long, gleaming metal shaft, with a tapered sort of rectangular end. It looked suspiciously like a golf club.

Wavy lines and red splotches appeared in front of my eyes; the sound in the room became strange, underwater, kind of like *whoom-whoom-whoom,* pounding in my ears. Through the stars and whooming I saw Carrot Top lean his horrible face and brown teeth into mine, his stinking breath and spittle robbing me of what little breath I had left. I was pushing against the club with all I had, but the combination of his superior strength and better angle meant I couldn't stop him from killing me.

He hissed at me, pools of foam collecting in the corners of his rancid mouth, pushing down on my throat with each word:

"*Where...is...the...money*?"

"Stop it! You'll kill him!"

Aria took one of those delicate feet and smashed her sandal into the side of his head, again and again. This shocked Carrot Top enough that he let up pressure on my neck. Then he stood up and turned toward her, and lifted the club like he was going to tee off on her skull. Aria fell back onto the mattress, terrified. "Bert! Help me!"

Something wrapped around Carrot Top's face. I was still on the brink of unconsciousness, but it looked like some kind of octopus had just swallowed his head. My eyes focused briefly and I saw purple, and some kind of shimmering silver stars and moons. Then the arms maneuvered Carrot Top into a headlock, and I saw Aku standing behind him, looking like some crazy Rasputin character, eyes wild and beard all frizzed out, wrestling my attacker in his wizard robe. Aku had the punk in a pretty serious hold, almost lifting him off his feet. It looked like Aku was trying to walk Carrot Top backwards, to get him out of the room, but Carrot Top wasn't exactly helpless; he got traction and backpedaled furiously, taking advantage of Aku's backward tilt and ramming him into the wall, which caused the resident wizard to drop his grip long enough for Carrot Top to bolt out of the room and down the stairs.

Aria dropped to her knees and put her hands on me. "Stay there," she said. "I'll call an ambulance."

"No...fine...help...bed..."

"Are you sure?"

I rubbed my throat and blinked once for yes. Aku and Aria helped me to the cot. Aria stroked my hair and forehead. I struggled to prop myself onto my elbows, coughed several times. "You okay?"

Aria rubbed her foot. "I think I jammed my toe when I kicked that dirt bag in the head, but I'm all right. Who the hell was that?"

"Corky Healey's killer."

Aria reached for her purse. "I'm calling the cops."

I stopped her. "Not yet. I need time to think."

"What's to think about? He tried to kill you, and me too for that matter! He would have succeeded if not for this nice man." Aku was pleased at the acknowledgment and bowed.

"I just need some time to think," I said. "Once the blood starts circulating again in my brain."

Aria combed my hair with her fingers. It was a feeling I could never get tired of. "Take your time," she said. "I won't call until you say." She looked at Aku. "Right?"

Aku bowed again. "Of course. I will trust you two to make the proper arrangements with the authorities; however, I am available if they should need a statement. Now if you'll excuse me, I think I will go downstairs and make sure the premises are secured." And with that he transported out and was gone. Aria turned to me and gave a little smirk.

"Strange character. What's his name?"

"Aku the Mystic."

"Does he always dress like that?"

"Pretty much."

"You certainly lead an interesting life. Can you get up? Lunch is on me."

I tried to sit. Bad idea. The combination of the fall, plus the weight of a one hundred and fifty pound man on my chest, trying to decapitate me with a steel club, had made my existing injuries much worse, while causing new problems. Rockets of pain went screaming and exploding across my neck and shoulders. I dropped back onto the mattress, my face a sour cactus of agony. "Arrr," I groaned. "Ah-ah-ah—"

"Bert!"

Aria was over at my side in an instant. "What can I do?"

"I was already injured," I gasped between sobbing bursts of blinding pain. "Just get me two aspirin and some water."

Aria found the aspirin and a plastic cup, which she filled with water from the jug by the bed, then gently placed the two tablets in my mouth. She helped me sip the water until I could swallow them.

"Looks like I'll have to take a rain check on our lunch date," I groaned. "You should go. I'll be fine."

"I'm not going anywhere. I'm staying right here until I know you're well enough to be on your own."

"I'm sorry for getting you involved in this—" She put her hand over my mouth.

"Are you kidding? This is the most excitement I've had since my first communion. You need your rest, plus something to eat." She looked around the room. "Where's the kitchen? Downstairs?"

I shook my head. "No kitchen."

"How do you cook?"

"I don't."

She looked stunned, not really comprehending. "You don't cook? How can you possibly live if you don't cook?"

"Chinese, pizza, burritos from 7-11."

Aria closed her eyes and shook her head, like she was trying to get the image out of her mind. "That's not food! That stuff will kill you!"

There was another knock on the door. "It's Aku," said the voice. Aria opened it a crack.

"I have checked the premises and bolted the front door from the inside. Since you and I are the only tenants at the moment, Bert, I figured you wouldn't mind."

"We're the only tenants? Guess that's why I haven't seen the other guys," I said drowsily.

"He's delirious," Aria said. "Aku, will you be here for a while?"

"I'm not planning on leaving my room until this evening," he said. "I have a meeting of the Elevens."

"What's that?"

"The Elevens are a race of Spirit Guardians who appear to us through the number eleven. If you've ever noticed your clock when it reads 11:11, for example, that's a sign that an angel is trying to talk to you."

"Hoo-kay." She cocked an eye at me, then got her bag. "I have some shopping to do. I'll be back in about an hour. Will you be sure to keep an eye on Bert while I'm gone?"

Aku bowed in that smooth way of his. "It would be an honor, my lady."

"I'm serious."

"So is he," I said.

"All right then." She came over and stroked my face with those delicate little fingers. "Just relax, dear. I'll be back soon with a feast. Aku, can I get you anything from the store?"

"No thank you, but it is very kind of you to offer. I shall follow you down and bolt the door." Aku flicked his hand and held something out to her. "Here is my card. Send me a text when you're a few blocks away, and I shall let you in."

Aria took the card. Their hands touched for a moment. Aku closed his eyes and smiled. "Yes, it is as I suspected. The spirit guardians are strong in you."

Aria gave me a what-the-hell look. "May the Force be with you too," she said. But I could tell by her smile that Aria was pleased. Besides, Aku was right. There was something so soothing and loving about Aria's touch that it was like a drug. Dr. K. had told me about something called hyper-vigilance, when you grow up with a lot of uncertainty and fear about the future so that you're always on guard, waiting for the next disaster, unable to relax. With Aria around, I felt so safe that I could finally relax, and sleep for a hundred years. The last thing I remember before I drifted off was murmuring, *You called me dear*, and then I was asleep.

When my eyes fluttered awake I saw Aria working busily at the desk. She had cleared off the typewriter and papers and was using it as a workstation, quietly and expertly slicing and chopping things. She looked over at me and smiled.

"I hope I didn't wake you."

"No, I don't think so," I croaked. "How long was I out?"

"Almost two hours."

"Sorry."

"Don't be silly. The market took a little longer than I expected, then when I came back I just sat and watched you for a little while, then read a magazine that I bought at the Stop & Shop. Then I figured I might as well get started."

"What are you doing?"

"What does it look like? I'm making you a home-cooked meal. I wondered why you were shoveling the food down so fast last night at the reception. Now I know."

"That's sweet," I said. "Wait a minute. How can you cook when I don't have a kitchen?"

She spun around and flung her arms out toward the opposite wall. "Ta-da!"

The top of the dresser was also cleared off. There was a small electric hot plate, with a pot of water beginning to steam on one burner and a smaller pot sitting on the other. Next to that was a toaster oven.

"I just got you a few things you needed." She saw the expression on my face. "Okay, so maybe you don't need them. But I do. At least, I do if I'm going to be spending more time here in the future."

"I'd rather take you out."

She scrunched her nose. "Half those places use canned tomatoes."

"What's wrong with that?"

"Watch and learn, altar boy."

I watched, but I still don't know how she did it. Aria was a factory of efficiency: slicing and chopping, combining and mixing, peeling and separating. The stale air in the room was soon filled with warm, homey smells. She mixed cheese, cream, and spices in a bowl. She kept running to and from the little dorm fridge, which was crammed with ingredients. I lay on the cot, watching in amazement. After about half an hour of this Aria wiped her hands on one of the new dish towels she had bought.

"Okay, I think we're good for now. I'll finish up in a bit." She reached into a bag and pulled out a bottle of red wine and a new corkscrew.

"It'll take a while for the water to boil. I think we both deserve a drink."

"I'll drink to that."

"I've been thinking about the guy who attacked you. I'm worried about Mrs. Healey. If that guy had something to do with her husband's death, she might be in danger."

I hadn't thought of that. "Hand me the phone. I'll call information and get her number."

She shook her head. "I tried that already. Unlisted. I'd call my dad for it but he'd start asking questions."

"Tell you what. I'll go over there in a little while and make sure she's all right."

"No."

"Why not?"

"*You're* not going over there. *We* are."

"Right." I grinned like an incontinent polar bear. We clinked glasses. The wine was good if you're into that kind of thing, then she got up to finish cooking.

I didn't always live like a caveman. I've eaten at some nice restaurants and had some good grub in my life. But I can honestly say that the meal that Aria prepared was the most delicious food I had ever tasted. It seemed simple, just pasta with a kind of tomato cream sauce, and a loaf of Italian bread that we tore hunks off of. There was a side of broccoli rabe with garlic and oil. It didn't look like much, but there was a touch, a kind of invisible magic that went into cooking, that made it an art. And Aria had that magic touch, the same that I felt when she touched me.

We ate in silence. There was nothing for us to say. The food did all the talking. When we were done Aria gathered the pots and dishes and silverware, and put them into a couple of shopping bags. "I'll bring these home to wash, then I can return them."

"Aria, that was amazing. I don't know how to thank you."

"My pleasure."

"Aren't your parents going to wonder where you are?"

"No. I told them I was going to be out most of the day and maybe tonight. They don't keep tabs on me every minute, just the big things, like how I spend the rest of my life. And with my sister's drama going on they wouldn't notice if I was there or not." She suddenly looked very sad.

"What's wrong?"

"Oh, nothing," she said, flashing those brown saucers at me. "It's just that I've been here for hours and you haven't even tried to kiss me yet."

Really

Hello, Love? It's me, Bert. I'm just letting you know that I have moved. I no longer live on Sad Sack Lane. My new address is Happiness Street, c/o Strawberry Fields, infinity plus forever. Please tell the spirit guardians that the angel they sent to protect me has arrived. Thank you. Signed, me.

I took Aria's fresh, mooning face in both hands and kissed her as if my life depended on it. She responded slowly at first, and then with more and more passion until things were hot and heavy. I could have kissed her forever. She was the best kisser in the world, period. It was more than kissing—we were having some crazy, deep conversation without words. It was like nothing else I had ever experienced or probably would again.

"I've been praying every day that I might find the right man," Aria said when we finally came up for air. "Someone I can have a real connection with, a soul mate. When I saw you in the church that day, hiding in the doorway and looking at me, I knew it was the answer to my prayers."

"Mine too, and I don't even pray."

She stroked my cheek as she whispered in my ear.

"I have a feeling I'm going to have to go to confession again, real soon."

She tried kissing me again but I pulled away.

"What's wrong?"

"I have to go to the bathroom so bad I might burst. I'll be right back."

"I'll be here," she purred. "Do you need help?"

"I can manage."

I limped across the hall and did my business in the filthy john. I was very glad that I had bought new underwear and sheets, at least. When I finished I washed my hands, shook them dry, and looked at myself in the mirror. There was a purple bruise across my throat, a painful reminder of my second run-in with that lunatic. I looked haggard and tired, but I also had a kind of scruffy raggedness that I thought was pretty cool. I went back across the hall and gently opened and closed the door. "Where were we?"

Aria was sitting on the bed. Except she wasn't smiling any more, and her look was anything but inviting. She looked up at me with a horrified expression, then back down at her lap. There, in her delicate hands, was the pink wedding purse.

She pushed past me and ran down the steps, sobbing. I went after her. We reached the car at the same time and I blocked the door.

"Get away from me, you dirt bag!"

She moved fast. She slapped me so hard that it almost knocked me off my feet. My other injuries only magnified the pain. I wobbled halfway across the road, sticking my legs out every way, trying to stay upright.

"God, what an *idiot* I am. You really had me going. I actually *believed* you and your stupid lies."

"It's not what you think!"

"No?" She held up the satchel. "So I guess I'm *imagining* this? Did it just appear *magically* in your drawer?"

"No, but—"

"Is that why you almost ran down my cousin, trying to get away? Is that why you didn't say anything to me about it all day, while I was shopping and cooking for you? Is that why that guy came charging in, demanding to know where *the money* was? You're not only a thief, you double-cross your accomplices too, is that it? No *wonder* you didn't want me to call the police! God, I was so stupid!"

"It doesn't look good, I know—"

She jabbed her finger at me. "*Shut* up. I don't want to hear it. Now let me go."

"You have to believe me. I found the bag in my car last night and I panicked. And I swear I was going to tell you about it. I was on my way over to your house when you showed up."

"I thought you were on your way to lunch."

"Right. I meant after lunch."

"You're pathetic."

"I'm not a criminal, Aria."

Her eyes narrowed in hatred. "I thought that's *exactly* what you are."

I had no comeback for that. It went through me like a knife. I jabbed my finger back at her.

"Oh yeah? Don't act all innocent with me, sister. You were using me this whole time too."

"Me? You're crazy."

"Am I? The second I walked out of my room to use the bathroom you went through my drawers, looking for evidence. How do you explain *that*?"

She shook her head. "You are so wrong."

"Then what were you looking for?"

"Nothing."

"See? At least I have a plausible excuse, even if you're too stubborn to see it. That's more than you've got."

Aria sighed.

"I was looking for protection," she said softly. I rolled my eyes.

"Like I would really hurt you. Nice try."

She gave me a look. "Not *that* kind of protection, dumbass. The other kind. I was going to give you the most special gift a woman can give, which I have been saving for the right man." She folded her arms and looked away. "I can't believe what an idiot I am. Another minute and I would have done something I would have regretted forever."

I cleared my throat.

"Aria, we seem to have gotten off on the wrong foot here. Can we just start over, and talk about this like reasonable adults?"

"No. I'm going home. Excuse me."

"Aria, think! Why would I try stealing something that would get me thrown into prison, or even worse? The cops can lock me up if I so much as jaywalk!"

"I don't know and I don't care. Maybe you owe people money. Maybe you're a drug addict. Maybe you get off on hurting women. All I know is, you broke my heart, Bert Shambles. I hope you're very happy with yourself. Now please get away from the car so I can leave, or you really *will* have a problem on your hands."

"Problem? Like the one your brothers gave me last night? And all those goons doing the security, intimidating people, making everybody feel like criminals? You faint when people do something bad to you, but you don't give anybody else the benefit of the doubt." I stepped out of the way. "Do your worst. I have nothing to hide. Have a nice night."

Some of what I said must have hit the target, because Aria didn't get in the car right away. She looked up at the sky, fighting back a new round of tears. She spoke very calmly and quietly.

"You're right, my family isn't nice. We're not good people. And I do like to have it both ways." The tears began running down her cheeks. "I know you didn't steal the money, Bert, but it still doesn't excuse you for...using me like that."

"Come back upstairs and we'll talk about it."

"No. I'm very tired and confused. I need time to think. But I'll make you a deal." She handed me the purse. "If you want me to trust you again, then you bring this to my house, tonight, and you explain to my father exactly what happened. He's a reasonable man, and I'll make sure nobody hurts or bothers you. That will prove to me that you are honorable, and then we'll see. No promises, except for your safety. Deal?"

"Deal."

"Really?"

"Of course. You're worth it."

I could see she was trying not to smile; her cheeks dimpled and the corners of her mouth turned up slightly. "Come between eight and nine."

I bowed. "I will be there, my lady."

"Aku does that better," she said.

A few minutes before eight I pulled onto Pondington Farms Road and began the long, slow drive to the Healey house. The wedding purse was on the seat next to me. My plan was to make sure Mrs. Healey was all right and tell her about Carrot Top, then head over to the Tortura house and get fitted for a pair of cement shoes. I didn't care what happened to me anymore; the pain of betrayal in Aria's eyes was something I couldn't live with. And her lips were something I couldn't live without.

I was about to pull in when I saw a pair of headlights turning onto the street from the other end of the semi-circular driveway. I rolled down my window the rest of the way and waved. I realized too late that the headlights did not belong to any car that Mrs. Healey would drive. They were attached to an old, battered white van.

The van stopped alongside and I saw that shock of red hair and nasty, freckled face glaring down at me. The mouth of the face moved and made a series of nasty words. I didn't stick around long enough to continue the conversation. I floored the Olds and she rumbled loudly up the street.

I checked the side mirror and saw that the van's brake lights were on. Then the white reverse lights came on and I almost fainted. I knew that the street ended in a dead end, and if Carrot Top knew that too then I was dead. I held my breath for what seemed like forever. Then the reverse lights went off, and the van kept going.

I had to pull over and catch my breath. My hands were shaking so badly now that I could barely hold the wheel. I thought about Mrs. Healey—was I already too late? Was she lying in a pool of blood inside the house? I did a three-point turn and went back to the Healey house. I left the engine running, in case Carrot Top decided to come back. I got out and rang the bell. No answer. I peered into the two narrow windows on either side of the door, but the glass was frosted and all the lights were off inside so I couldn't see anything.

The sound of a car engine revving almost gave me a heart attack. Another car came out from behind the house, from where the garage was. It was moving so fast that the front end scraped on the bottom lip of the driveway. It was a black Mercedes, but unlike any I had seen. It looked more like the Batmobile, one of those ultra-expensive models.

I went around the side of the house and down the driveway. I remembered the door code that Dale punched into the keypad. I thought I should go inside and see if Mrs. Healey was okay, but knowing my luck, the cops would arrive just as I was leaning over her dead body. Another thought hit me: what if Mrs. Healey and Carrot Top were in cahoots somehow? If so, then why would she make a stink about her husband being murdered? It didn't make sense.

I ran back to the Olds, jumped in and gunned it. I no longer cared about the speed limit; the other cars had a big lead, but the 442 was more than happy to give chase. I was doing 50 in a 25 zone, and enjoying it quite a bit. The wind howled into the open window and whipped my hair around. It was a couple of miles to the intersection with Mumfrey

Boulevard; if I didn't catch them by then there would be no way to tell which way they went. In spite of my anxiety and fear, I laughed as the Olds roared through the night.

I caught up to the van and car just as they were turning left onto the Boulevard. I gunned it one more time as the light turned yellow and then red, screeched wildly around the corner about a second too late and just missed being hit by a lady in an Escalade. I brought my speed down to the posted limit and tried to catch my breath.

The glass of the Mercedes was tinted and there were almost no markings, except for a white oval sticker on the rear bumper that said 'STK.' I had Daddy-O's pen but couldn't find any paper to write down the license plate number. By the time I thought of writing it on my hand the Mercedes made a sudden right onto Harbor Road. I didn't know which car to follow. If I followed the van, I might find out where Carrot Top lived, and maybe find out enough information to give to the police when I reported him. I didn't know who was in the other car. It could be Dorothy or Dale Healey, but it could also be a gang of thugs working with Carrot Top. I decided to take the poison I knew; I followed the van.

We drove south on Mumfrey Boulevard for seven or eight miles, until we reached the service road for the L.I.E. heading west. Traffic moved well, and I followed the van easily for the next thirty or forty minutes, until we took the exit for the Grand Central Parkway. We stayed on that for a few more miles until we got off at an exit I was unfamiliar with. We were somewhere in Queens, I knew that much. The skyline of Manhattan looked close enough to touch. The van made another turn and I saw signs that told me we were in Astoria.

It wasn't long before I remembered why I never drive into Queens if I can avoid it. The roads confuse the hell out of me. We crossed 30th Avenue, then 30th Road, then 30th Drive, then turned left and soon we crossed 30th Street. It made no sense. I stopped looking at the signs and concentrated on following the van. There was the usual mix of commerce and residential, bars and bodegas, signs advertising things in Greek and Korean and Spanish. I didn't know where the hell I was.

The van finally turned onto a dismal little block, mostly desolate-looking low brick buildings housing various light industry: chop shops, meth labs, Ukrainian prostitutes, and everything else. The van swung into a space and I parked about a dozen lengths behind. Carrot Top took no notice of me. He crossed the street and went into a nondescript place with a neon sign in the window that said *Billiards*.

I shut off the car, found a pen and a scrap of paper and walked over to the van and wrote down the details, the make and model and license plate number. There were two bumper stickers, on the back, and I wrote them down: one said I BREAK FOR POOL and the other said POOL PLAYERS HAVE 8 BALLS.

I peered in through one of the side windows. I couldn't see what was back there, it was too dark, but it looked like some kind of tarp or blanket was covering something else, something underneath that was shaped like a mound. Almost like a body.

I ran back to the Olds, and found an old wire hanger on the floor. I untwisted it, made a hook, then went to the passenger door on the van and started fishing. It was an old van, so I guessed it would probably work the same way that it did with the Olds. I was right. The hanger caught the mechanism and I pulled. There was a clunking sound and the button popped up. I opened the door a crack and slipped inside.

There was a little ledge between the two seats, with some papers on it. I took them and put them in my pocket, to go through later. There was some change, too, but I left it. I climbed into the back. The floor was soft. I looked closer and saw the floor was filled with black plastic garbage bags. I reached into one and pulled out a pair of pink polyester golf pants, with the tags still on. I looked through the rest and found more of the same. Either it was Corky Healey's donation, or there was a secret society devoted to ugly clothing.

I groped around in the semi-darkness, but there was no body, no Mrs. Healey. I felt something cold, and pulled a golf club out from under the bags. It looked like the one Carrot Top had used to choke me. I was pretty sure it was the missing putter. I looked closer. I was right. Along the metal shaft there was some writing engraved into it. I had to squint to make it out. It said, *Property of Corky Healey.*

I heard a noise from the front of the van. I had just enough time to slide down the wall and partially hide under the bags as the driver's side door opened and Carrot Top got in. He started the engine and we pulled away from the curb.

No

We drove for a long time, with lots of turns along the way. I tried to keep track of the lefts and rights but gave up after a while. The exhaust fumes were strong in the back of the van; it took all my effort to keep from throwing up. Carrot Top tuned the radio to one of those new rock stations that played bands with names like Fludge and Strep and Meatböll, and all the singers sounded like the Cowardly Lion in *The Wizard Of Oz*. That didn't help matters.

The van finally stopped. Carrot Top cut the engine and got out. As soon as the door slammed I got myself up and into position. I hoped he was going away, but I had to be ready. I went for the surprise attack. I crouched behind the rear doors, choked up on the putter like it was a baseball bat. I heard the key in the lock. The bags were piled around me, my footing was unsteady, but when the doors opened I roared like some crazy tribal warrior.

Carrot Top slipped as he jumped back, and clocked his head on the hard metal edge of the roof. He landed hard on the hood of the car parked behind the van, bounced off and hit the ground with a thud.

I jumped out and raised the club over my head. He held his arms up in a cross in front of his face and started whimpering.

"Don't hurt me, man! Take whatever you want, but don't hurt me!"

"How do you like it, asshole? Not so much fun, is it? Why are you following me? Tell me or I'll smash you!"

Carrot Top was curled into a fetal position, arms wrapped around his head. He was shaking all over. "How did you ff-find me?"

"I know everything about you, slime ball. That is, everything except why you have the clothes, or this golf club, or why you're hanging around with Bill Shanley, or what happened to Mr. and Mrs. Healey. But I know everything else."

"The cl-clothes," he stammered. "S-something in the p-p-pockets."

"*What's* in the pockets?"

"Something that belongs to me!"

"What?"

"I don't know. Really!"

I lifted the club. "You think that's funny?"

"Money! I think it was supposed to be a lot of money."

"You *think*?"

"I don't know, I swear. He died before I could find out. I just know that he said it was in one of his pockets, but they were empty."

"When was this?"

"At the golf course. I saw him die, man! I was supposed to meet him there and when I got there he was in a ditch."

"What's Bill Shanley's role in all this? Don't bother denying it, because I saw the two of you on the beach, getting onto his boat."

"You did? Oh man, oh man. He said that if anyone found out about that then the deal was off."

"What deal?"

"My share. I can't say any more. But he said he would match whatever the old man gave me, plus a lot more. That's why I wanted the clothes."

"Because when you couldn't find what you were looking for in the dead man's pockets, you decided to search the rest of his wardrobe, is that right?"

Carrot Top nodded frantically. "He had me pose as a driver from the Goodwill, to pick up the clothes. But when I got there, he texted me that I should wait, there was a complication."

"Texted? You mean, you have a cellphone?"

"Sure man, doesn't everybody?"

"Never mind."

"I was waiting for the signal to come up to the house but I got lost on my way over there and was late. That's when you came by and picked up the bags. So I followed you until I could get them back."

"If you were so worried about the clothes then why did you start with me in the bar?"

"Oh man, I was just pissed off. I heard you talking to that fine redhead about how you were doing some secret job for Mrs. Healey, and I thought maybe she was playing me and Mr. Shanley for some kind of fools, then I couldn't figure out why she'd hire such a loser to do her dirty work for her and I just snapped."

"Loser, huh? Well, guess who's holding the golf club now, Jethro?"

"I know, man! I know! I'm just saying, that's the kind of crazy thoughts I was having."

"What have you done to Mrs. Healey?"

"Nothing!" He laughed bitterly. "Nobody could do nothing to her, and I pity the guy who tries."

"Why were you at her house?"

"You'll have to ask her, man. You can crack my skull open, but I'm not saying any more until I see a lawyer. I've had it with all you crazy people."

"Is that why you killed Corky Healey?"

"I didn't, I swear!"

"Then what are you doing with his golf club?"

"It was lying next to him when I got there. I took it because I needed something to help me get out of that pit, it was too slippery for me to climb up in my boots."

"It never occurred to you that this might be a murder weapon? You took evidence from the scene of a potential crime and didn't report it to the police?"

"And tell them what? That I just happened to be walking along a private golf course early in the morning? Think anyone would have believed me?"

I hated to admit it, but for once I could understand where Carrot Top was coming from. It was the type of situation that I had found myself in more than once.

"But don't you know that makes you an accomplice after the fact, or at the very least, guilty of obstructing justice?"

I wasn't sure if what I said was accurate or not, but watching all those British mysteries on PBS at least helped me sound like I knew what I was talking about. Carrot Top just groaned and held his head.

"HEY!"

I looked over my left shoulder. There was an old man standing by a fence, just a few feet down the sidewalk, looking right at me. The club was still in my hand, held like an axe about to come down on Carrot Top's head.

"What the hell's going on there?"

I did the only sensible thing I could think of. I took off and ran like hell.

I went at full speed for several blocks, until I thought my heart would explode. My breath came in gulps and big hysterical wheezes, like I was choking on air. I couldn't stop. I had to keep moving, in any direction. I had no idea where I was until a jet screamed overhead, a big passenger plane, and I realized that I was near LaGuardia airport.

I came to an intersection. I still had no idea which way to go, especially given the crazy street numbers that crisscrossed all over the place. Diagonally across the street I saw a big, official-looking sign. I crossed over for a better look. The sign confirmed what I thought: I was on the road to Rikers Island.

I started jogging again.

As I zigzagged through the streets, only one thing brightened my mood: the look on Carrot Top's face. Seeing him lying there, cowering and whimpering, begging for mercy, gave me a real sense of accomplishment. On that level, at least, the adventure had been a success.

But I still didn't know what Carrot Top had been trying to tell me. This was a job for a brilliant criminal mind, like one of those British detectives they always show on PBS. What would DCI Barnaby do? I was way out of my league.

I got to 20th Avenue. I remembered parking somewhere near 30th Avenue, or maybe 30th Street or 30th Lane. Whatever it was, as long as the numbers kept going up I was reasonably sure I would find my way back.

One more thing worried me: Carrot Top had recognized me as he pulled away from the Healey house; by now he must have figured out that I followed him to Queens and broke into his van while he was in the billiards place. If that were the case, then he would know that I had to be parked somewhere near there. Maybe he would call his buddies in the pool hall and have them waiting outside, keeping watch. I didn't want to think what they would do to me if they caught me.

I found a bar with a pay phone near the intersection of Ditmars and Steinway. The bouncer pointed to the putter and said it qualified as a weapon. I pulled out my wallet and showed him Daddy-O's card and said it was evidence in a police case and that I had to "phone it in." He was cool after that. I got change from the bartender, found the payphone and dialed. I got his voicemail. I preferred leaving a message, since I really didn't want to talk to him. He and Devil Girl were probably out "cutting a rug" or "grooving" to some band. He had to be a dozen years older than her. It was indecent and infuriating and I couldn't think about it or I would go insane.

Daddy-O's outgoing message said that he would be out of the office until after the holiday, and that if it was an emergency to call 911 or else leave a message after the beep. I plugged my ear and had to speak loudly to be heard over the noise. I said that I had information about a possible murder, involving a white van with Louisiana plates, and that he should call me at home as soon as possible. When I hung up I felt better. I gave the bouncer a five on my way out and thanked him. He wished me luck in the investigation. He even called me *Officer*. As much as I hate to admit it, the momentary rush of power was a total buzz.

What was I worried about? What was Carrot Top going to do? Even if I still couldn't prove anything, he didn't know that. There was something shady going on, and he was part of it. If I had scared him properly, and I thought I had, I had nothing to worry about.

I didn't know why anyone would want to kill a 91-year old golfer just to steal his ugly clothes. Maybe the competition for hip vintage golf outfits was worse than Cassie realized.

After a lot more walking and confusion, I finally found the street. I was so tired that I didn't care anymore who was waiting for me. The billiards sign was turned off; I crossed the street and looked into the lone, small window. It looked like pool tables, all right. A sign in the window said Sales, Repairs, & Service.

My car was still there, half a block down. No sign of the van anywhere. The Olds started on the first try. I put her into drive and started looking for the way back.

I got home around midnight. I had never been so tired. I remembered Aria, and my promise to her, but I hoped she would understand when I saw her again. I didn't even have her number. I had been so confident that I would show up at her place that I hadn't bothered to get it from her. The last thing she had said to me was that I would regret it if I didn't show, or that she couldn't be held responsible for what happened to me, something like that. But if I started letting her dictate everything in the relationship right from the beginning then it would only get worse as time went on.

I took the golf club and the empty wedding purse and dragged myself upstairs. The driving, the running, the stress of seeing Carrot Top again. I got upstairs and was about to open my door when Aku appeared in the hallway, carrying a candle in a wild brass holder that looked like a coiled dragon, with the candle stuck in its mouth.

"Is everything all right?"

"I hope so."

"Bert, I was thinking about that man who was in your room. I'm very concerned for your safety."

"Thanks, but it's over. I don't think he'll be coming back here." I lifted the putter. "I've taken care of it."

"I see. Is that what I think it is?"

"It depends on what you think *it* is, but yes, it is."

Aku gazed at me with those intense eyes, as he stroked his beard with one hand and the candlelight flickered wild shadows on the walls.

"I threw the tarot for you earlier; I hope you don't mind. I tried to divine something of your future in the cards."

"What did they say?"

His eyes got wide all of a sudden; he stared off into space. His expression was frozen. The candle got very dim for a few seconds, then the flame flared up once, very large, before sizzling and sputtering and settling down again. It freaked me the hell out. Aku came out of the trance. He looked at me.

"What just happened?"

"I don't know. You were saying something about my future, then bugged out."

"I did? Strange. It happens sometimes when I am receiving a particularly strong signal."

"What signal? What happens?"

He closed his eyes and then opened them. He spoke in a strange monotone.

"There is a chance of thunderstorms later. Make sure your car windows are rolled up. Good night."

The candle flickered again and he was gone.

I went into my room. That was his big insight? A weather forecast? If that's how the scam worked then the people who called him for advice were even stupider than I thought. He was a lousy weather man, too. On the drive home I had listened to the news and they kept saying how the whole area was going to have clear, beautiful weather all week. The overnight forecast was clear.

I got my toothbrush and toothpaste and brought them across the hall to the bathroom. As I brushed I heard something. It sounded like a clap of thunder. I spit out the toothpaste and tried opening the bathroom window. It was stuck because of the humidity, but with a bit of pushing and banging I got it open and looked out. Nothing but stars.

Strange. I tried pulling the window back down but it was jammed, and I was too tired to deal with it. I went back into my room, kicked off my shoes and lay on top of the covers and closed my eyes.

Another clap of thunder.

Maybe it was some kids shooting off their fireworks a few days early. Maybe some sudden, freak thunderstorm had appeared out of nowhere. I didn't know if my car windows were open or not. I peeked out the tattered little curtain at the Olds. The windows were closed. I was about to forget it and go to sleep for the next twelve hours when a large white Cadillac with its headlights off rolled very slowly up to the rooming-house.

The driver was obviously making an effort to be very quiet; if I hadn't been looking out at that moment I never would have heard. The doors of the Caddy opened silently, and the Tortura boys piled out. It was eighty degrees outside. They were all wearing leather gloves.

I don't know when I've ever moved so fast. I jammed my feet into my unlaced shoes and opened my door a crack. I could hear them fidgeting with the front door. They were whispering in that way that meatheads have, where they were trying to make sure that people heard them whispering. They seemed to be having some kind of argument, which I assumed was about whether or not they should just break in. I heard the knob being tested, then a push-push-crack as they forced the door open with brute strength.

The only way out.

I looked across the hallway to the bathroom. I could see the open window. It was small, but it was my only chance. I bolted across the hall and closed and locked the bathroom door just as their heavy feet stormed up the stairs. I heard them talking outside the bathroom door, about what to do to me. One of the brothers said that he thought the whole thing was stupid, that I wasn't worth it. I hoped maybe they would have a change of heart. Another voice asked which door they should try first, then another noticed that my door was open a crack. There was a knock, a big voice said hello, then I heard a yell:

"You guys, over here! Look! He's still got Angela's wedding purse, sitting on his floor!"

Damn.

This set off a volcano of enraged reactions from the four Tortura boys, ranging from "I'm gonna kill him" to "I'm gonna rip his face off" and everything in between. No time to lose. I got onto the edge of the filthy tub, put one knee on the sink and my hands on the windowsill. I didn't trust the sink to hold my weight, so I rocked back and forth a few times then pushed up and forward with one gymnastic sort of motion. The old sink groaned and made a cracking sound. The doorknob started jiggling like crazy.

I pulled myself through the window to my waist then wiggled the rest of the way onto the lower roof that extends to the back of the first floor. I landed with a thud and scrambled down to the edge of the roof, where there was a small maple that I could shimmy across. The bathroom door made a sickening noise as it burst open. The light went on, flooding most of the roof, including me. I made a wild leaping grab for the branch, caught hold, but felt one of my shoes drop into the darkness. I pulled myself along the branch for a few feet, then let myself drop onto the moist earth below. I scanned for my shoe but it was pitch black. The Tortura boys were stomping down the stairs, coming for me. I ran wildly into the darkness of the yard and climbed the overgrown old fence at the rear of the property, the rusty links cutting into my toes and the unfinished pointy tips running along the top of the fence digging into my groin and butt as I pulled myself over.

Awesome

I hacked blindly through the dark underbrush, getting shredded by thorns and whipped in the face with small branches as gross, wet things soaked my socks and sharp sticks and rocks made me yelp in pain until I twisted my ankle.

There was a little embankment down to a bed of large gravel, then I crossed the train tracks, a few hundred feet from the station. I reached the edge of the platform, calculated what appeared to be the shortest distance across the lot, then ran the best I could with only one shoe until I reached cover on the other side. I ran-limped down the dark residential side streets, making my way back up to Mumfrey Boulevard. Once I crossed that I would be back in the relative safety of darkness, but I had to cross it first.

I stood behind a large tree a few houses back from the main road and considered my options. I could call a cab back at the train station, but it would mean crossing the open expanse of the parking lot and making the call in plain view, and then waiting ten or twenty minutes. There was an Italian restaurant down a few blocks, and a gas station a couple of blocks the other direction that might have a phone, but everything between was just various little shops and services, accountants and optometrists, nail salons and travel agents, all closed. My only chance was Mother MacCree's.

It's a dirty little place, the last live-music joint in Mumfrey, a rundown relic of the 1970s when bikers roared down the streets and there were some cool things in town: head shops selling bongs and papers for potheads, music shops with black light posters and vinyl LPs, places that sold incense and hippie clothes with lots of suede fringe and Native American designs. I've asked my mom about those times because they seem so alien now, living in a world where people think websites are cool. I'm sure people back then were just as bored and shallow as they are now, but I can't really say that we've made much progress, either. I didn't know if there was a pay phone in the place, but at least there were people. Maybe the bartender would let me use the phone. I could tell him I lost my shoe, because I did; it was an emergency.

A group walked up to the corner, three guys and two girls, waiting to cross. They looked roughly my age, though it was hard to tell because they were so clean-cut. The girls were making last minute adjustments to hair and lips, the guys joked and joshed. I waited until the light was about to change, then hop-ran right up behind them, close enough to blend in but not so close that they noticed.

The light changed and we all walked across as a group. A big vinyl sign hung outside the pub, advertising a new brand of light beer and the name of the night's entertainment: Shattered Dreams, playing the best classic rock hits. Ten-cent chicken wings and dollar drafts all night. A perfect evening of Long Island culture. As we reached the front door, I looked over my shoulder and saw a slow-moving Cadillac coming down the street.

Tortura boys hung out of the rear windows, one on each side, scanning the street and sidewalk. One of them spotted me. He pointed excitedly and shouted something to the others.

"Excuse me," I said to the group ahead of me, "I have an emergency situation." The guys looked at me and their faces kind of went strange. To my surprise one of them said "Sure, go ahead," and I thanked him. As I cut in front I heard one of the girls say, *Oh my God, what's wrong with that guy?* Which in my experience is never a good sign. I pulled out my wallet and showed it to the doorman, who also looked at me strangely.

I asked if the bar had a pay phone and he jerked his thumb.

"In the back. But I'm not sure it still works." I thanked him and then I thought of something else.

"Some big guys just roughed me up and mugged me," I said. "I'm really scared they might still be after me. I'm just calling a cab and then I'll be out of here." The doorman nodded and I went in.

Mother MacCree's is a decent-sized place, and it was crowded. It was difficult to maneuver, especially with one wet sock that was sticking to the beer and chicken grease caked on the floor. My foot suctioned to the ground with each disgusting step, but that was better than getting my toes crushed by the drunk crowd that was swaying to the classic rock styling of Shattered Dreams. The singer was dressed in a kind of Robin Hood outfit, leggings and little booties, holding a flute. He made funny faces and did a crazy dance, then started singing something about park benches and little girls.

I looked behind me. A couple of the Tortura boys were arguing with the doorman, who must have figured out that these were the big guys I said had attacked me. I kept my head down while I wetsocked my way to the back of the room, to the side of the stage. Ahead of me was the hallway to the bathrooms, and at the end was a pay phone. Next to that was a metal fire door with a panic bar and a lighted EXIT sign hanging over it. I made it to the phone and lifted the receiver. It was dead. Dead as I was going to be in just another minute. I checked the exit door. There was no alarm. I pushed the bar and opened the door a crack. There was a landing, then some steps leading down to a small lot behind the club, with a Dumpster and some rusting old kitchen and bar equipment. There was a high fence that was overgrown with a tangle of unkempt bushes and topped with spirals of razor wire, and a gate leading to the street. The gate was open. I was about to make my move when I saw one of the Tortura boys near the gate, leaning against a car and staring calmly into space.

I closed the door quietly, before the light and noise spilling from the club gave me away. I went into the men's room, heart pounding. There was a guy at the urinal, his head tilted back in a drunk semi-stupor as he muttered something to himself and peed half onto the floor. I envied him. Then the drunk abruptly finished and stumbled out. He didn't wash his hands.

I went over to the sink and looked at myself in the streaked and cracked mirror that was mostly covered with band stickers and unreadable tags done with Sharpie pens. Now I knew why the people at the entrance had looked so shocked: I had twigs and leaves in my hair, streaks of dirt and blood across my face, like I was wearing some crazy tribal camouflage. Even a few stray thorns stuck here and there.

I knocked the twigs and leaves out of my hair and rubbed water on my face, then reached for a towel. It was one of those old, continuous feed machines with a roll of actual cloth inside, where you pull down a segment of fresh fabric and the used portion gets pulled up into the back of the dispenser. Or at least, that's how they're supposed to work. This one was stuck, and the part of towel that was showing was filthy. It wouldn't pull in either direction. Maybe it was at the end of the roll. I was going to die with a wet face and hands.

In a fit of desperation I yanked the towel, hard, and part of the dirty section pulled out of the back and ripped. I yanked it again, and the old towel ripped completely and hung down almost to the floor. I wiped my hands on my pants and dried my face on my sweaty and stinking T-shirt instead.

To the right of the sink I noticed a garbage can with a plastic liner. It was filled with beer cups and chicken wings and whatever else. An idea. It was a long shot, but I had nothing to lose. I pulled the plastic liner out of the can and made a knot in the top. Then I pulled the back of the used towel feed down even more, until I found another ripped spot in the fabric. I tore the towel completely off and wrapped the filthy thing around my waist like an apron. I tucked the two loose ends into the side of my jeans, then rolled up my T-shirt sleeves for added effect. I got my head under the faucet and soaked my hair and slicked it completely back. I picked up the garbage bag and headed out of the bathroom.

There was nobody in the hallway, except for a couple of women waiting for the other bathroom. I went to the exit door, took a deep breath. Confidence. It was only going to work if I acted confident. I knocked open the door with my hip and pushed my way out noisily and obviously, the garbage bag hoisted over my shoulder in such a way that my arms partially obscured my face. I walked down the steps and headed across the crunchy gravel to the Dumpster. I could feel the eyes of the Tortura goon on me from the street. I just hoped that he didn't notice my missing shoe. He didn't move. Casually I tossed the garbage bag into the bin, and picked up a few beer bottles and other pieces of garbage lying around. As I bent over I stole glances at the goon; he wasn't paying any attention to me now. He kept looking down the sidewalk, towards the main road, perhaps for a signal from one of the others.

I stood up, wiped my hands on the apron and walked out to the sidewalk. I acted like a man with time on his hands. I stretched, sighed loudly, and strolled a little ways up, as if checking the perimeter of the fence for any more loose trash. I bent and picked up some stray pieces of paper, whistling to myself.

And kept walking.

At the end of the block I started jogging. As I went past the neat little houses, I wondered if anyone else in Mumfrey spent as much time as I did trying to escape from hit men, goons, and gangsters. If so, then I hadn't run into them yet.

I made it to the dead-end, went around the metal barricade, and dropped safely down into another stretch of woods. There was a stream there, which I knew would lead me to the edge of a narrow but very dark and wooded park that would eventually open up to the duck pond. From there I would have to expose myself for about a quarter mile, until I got to another desolate stretch of woods. For the moment I was relatively safe.

I didn't know how to feel, exactly. I couldn't be angry with Aria, not really. When I hadn't shown up she had done what she thought was right, and ratted me out to her family. It was understandable, but I was still disappointed. There were a million reasons why I might not have shown up. For all she knew maybe Carrot Top had come back and killed me, or maybe Mrs. Healey was dead and I was down at the station, giving a statement to the police. For someone who still went to church regularly, even at her age, Aria obviously lacked faith. It was too late now.

The stream finally disappeared underground, I scrambled up a small hill and crossed a dark street, then picked up the path that would lead me to the duck pond. When I came out at the other end I couldn't jog or run any more so I walked the few hundred yards, around the back end of the pond and up the final steep hill. At the top was a row of houses, which continued down the other side of the hill. One of the first I came to was a humble brick and aluminum two-family house. I went around to the back. There was a ladder lying there, in the darkness. I lifted the ladder to the second floor, window on the left, climbed up, slid the window open and crawled inside.

Lovely

"Bert! What a nice surprise!"

"Good morning, mom."

"Morning? It's after two o'clock already!"

"I must have been more tired than I thought."

Mom is petite, about five-two and a hundred and change, soaking wet. She was quite beautiful as a younger woman and still is, but the years and worry and cheap wine have taken their toll. She's fifty-six, which means she had me at thirty-three, and my dad left a couple of years later. She was still quite beautiful even at thirty-five, so I don't know why she didn't meet some guy and get herself a companion. Instead she had gotten two baby kittens, Scram and Shoo, both of whom were now around twenty and looking more like a hundred. They shuffled, snorted, farted, twitched, belched, fell over sideways at random times, sometimes fell asleep mid-poop in the kitty litter, but they are the only three living creatures who I can remember being there for my entire life, and I was never so glad to see the three of them as I was that moment.

"What's wrong with your face?"

"I fell in a bush."

"I see. So what did I do to deserve the pleasure of your company?"

"Does a guy need an excuse to see his mom?"

"Of course not; I just haven't heard from you in a while and I was wondering if everything was all right."

"Things are fine."

"Are you going to stay for a while, or is it just a quick visit?"

"I thought I'd stay tonight if that's all right."

"It's wonderful, but I'll have to run out to the market. I don't have anything in the house to eat. Are you hungry?"

"A little." The truth was that I was starving, but I didn't want to do anything to confirm her belief that I couldn't take care of myself. "But it's not a big deal."

"You must need something, if you slept that late. I'll go to the market and then go to the deli and pick up a late lunch if that sounds good."

"Sounds great, thanks."

"How did you get in? I had the bolt on."

"I used the ladder and climbed in through my bedroom window."

She frowned. "Well, just be sure you put it away. I wouldn't want someone to climb in here and rob me out of house and home."

I looked around the living room. We had inherited most of the furniture from my grandmother. It was all at least 30 years old, and some of it twice as old as that. It had been nice in its day, but not anymore. Everything in the apartment was drooped and tattered, scarred by years of general use as well as the cats' endless claw-sharpening exercises, drool, and vomit. I wanted to ask her who in his right mind would steal that junk, but I let it pass.

"No work today?"

My mom grinned. "Nope. Vinnie's daughter is getting married, and since it's a short week anyway because of the holiday, he decided to close the office for the week. He's giving us our full pay, too. You could have knocked me over with a feather."

My mom has worked for a local attorney for the last fifteen years. That's how I was able to get represented at the trial. He's a decent enough guy, and has been pretty good to his employees over the years, but my mom still acts as if every little act of decency or kindness is some kind of miracle.

"What about you? What's happening at the store?"

"Not much. Things are quiet, especially while Fr. Pete is on vacation."

My mom nodded. "That's right. He has a sister with a place in the Berkshires, I think. Is everything all right?" She gave me The Eye, that look that tells me she thinks something is wrong even when nothing is. It's especially annoying when things aren't all right and I can't lie my way out of it smoothly.

"Of course," I said vaguely. "I'm fine. Why do you ask?"

"Nothing. Just that you usually call before you come over. And you look like you must have had quite a night. You're covered in scratches and have twigs in your hair."

"I was just goofing around with some friends."

She wasn't buying it for a second, but she knew better than to push me on the issue. "It must have been quite a party," she said finally.

I changed the subject. "Speaking of parties, I hear there's a big fundraiser at the Pondington Country Club."

"Oh yes, the charity golf tournament. I had forgotten. How do you know about that?"

"I heard it from Mrs. Healey, when I went over to pick up some clothes she donated to the thrift shop."

"As in, Corky Healey? You run with a swell bunch. He was such a handsome man, I recall. I never got a very warm feeling from his wife. She seemed very cold to me. She was very rude to me on the phone the other day."

"What do you mean?"

"I can't talk about it. You know the rules."

One thing I love about mom is that she's very, uh, scrupulous, I guess is the word. She doesn't discuss clients or anything else about work. But she also has this thing, about how every guy is secretly being controlled by some manipulative shrew. Every time someone in town gets engaged, married, divorced, or has a kid, mom makes some comment about how the poor guy is being led around by the nose. In her view, the world was full of gullible, weak, stupid men who were being dominated by crafty spouses bent on nothing but their misery. The hairs on my arms rose in defense, but I was too tired and sore to argue about it.

"Well, she was perfectly polite and friendly to me," I said curtly. "I only brought up the fundraiser because I know you and dad used to spend time at the club, years ago."

Her eyes were still faraway. "Yes, that's right. Bill Shanley does it every year, to raise money for some charity or another. It makes people forget what a skunk he is."

"You knew him pretty well?"

"Sure, and that whole gang from Pondington. Your father taught a lot of them how to sail." She shook her head. "Poor man."

"Who, dad?"

"No, Bill Shanley."

"I thought he was loaded."

"He is. But he's had a lot of tragedy in his life. He lost his wife in a terrible situation."

"What happened?"

"Didn't I ever tell you?"

"Not that I remember."

Mom took a deep breath. "Her name was Kathy. She was a beautiful woman, vibrant, so much fun. All the men were in love with her, including your father. She was a champion sailor, one of the best on the east coast. Well, one day she went out for a sail and didn't come back. They found the empty sailboat, floating out in the bay. They never found her body."

"That's terrible. So what happened?"

"Who knows? It was quite a big deal. Bill was a prime suspect, of course, but nothing ever came of it. I always thought there was something rotten about the whole thing. Back then a lot of people thought that Bill had something to do with it. I'm sure some of them still do." Mom shrugged. "There it is."

"Why did you all suspect him?"

"Well, because Bill had a motive. There was talk down at the club that Kathy was going to divorce him, because of his philandering. Bill always had a girlfriend, or two or three, and I guess she got sick of it. Kathy had all the money. She got Bill started in his business, with her deep pockets and powerful contacts. So he probably had the most to lose if she left him, and the most to gain if she died."

"In other words, it's nothing more than small-town gossip."

Mom stopped and gave me the hairy eyeball. "Why are you so interested in Bill Shanley all of a sudden?"

"Can't a guy be interested in people for a change?"

"Of course. But you've never shown any interest before. And you show up here with scratches all over your face and pretend like everything is normal. Is something going on that I don't know about?"

"Well, to tell you the truth, I think he might be involved in some bad stuff."

"What kind of bad stuff?"

"Corky Healey's death."

"Are you kidding? He must have been a hundred and two."

"Ninety-one, to be precise. I know it sounds crazy, but Mrs. Healey suspects foul play. And I've discovered other things that make me believe he might be involved."

"What kinds of things?"

"Nothing much. Just that he was hanging around with some real bad character the other night, at the Tortura wedding."

"Tortura? Talk about a rotten bunch. What were you doing there?"

"I had to serve mass, then Scotty asked me to help him at the reception, turning pages."

"You served the mass? Aren't you a little old to be an altar boy?"

"I wish people would stop asking me that. Anyway, I saw him down on the beach that night with a real shady character."

"On the beach? Is that where the wedding was?"

"No, I was down there with Aria, the youngest daughter."

"Those fat cows? What are you doing hanging around them?"

"She's not a fat cow, mom, or even a skinny cow. She's beautiful. We were in school together, and she's been a good friend to me lately. Will you please lay off the criticism?"

Mom got a faraway look and her eyes began to shine, like she was fighting back tears. I saw a box of Kleenex on the floor. I took one and handed it to her.

"What's wrong?"

She shook her head and blew her nose.

"Nothing. It just makes me sad, thinking of those days. We had some wonderful times back then, your father and I."

I knew mom wasn't telling me everything, but I also knew that there was nothing more I could say right then. Mom was gone, back to her favorite hangout, the Good Old Days. It seemed like all her happiest memories were before I was born, back where I couldn't share in them. Even worse, back before I came along and ruined everything. Sometimes I wish she would get over my dad leaving us and move on with her life, and stop making me feel like I was the reason. I suddenly remembered why I had found my own room across town.

I told mom what I wanted from the deli and she went. While she was gone I took a long, hot shower. I found an old pair of shoes in the closet. They were in bad shape, stiff and uncomfortable, but they were better than nothing.

Mom came back with a few bags from the market and the sandwiches. The dining table was covered with papers, old mail, and other clutter that was cleaned off once a year, at the holidays, and promptly put back as of January 1. We sat on the couch to eat, as usual. Mom's two ancient cats, Shoo and Scram, curled themselves into tight little balls against her hips, like two ratty, drooling, loud-snoring bookends. I had a turkey hero with lettuce and mayo, some chips and a Coke. Mom had roast beef on whole wheat with mustard and a glass of wine.

When we were done eating, I decided I needed a change of scene. I also needed some time to think about how to handle the situation with Aria, so she would call off her brothers. Now that they had found the purse in my room, and had proof, what if they decided to have the police handle the theft instead? I would be screwed.

"Can I borrow your car for a little while?"

"Of course, as long as you put some gas in it. Where's yours?"

"It's at home. It was running a little hot so I thought I'd take it into the shop."

"I see. Where are you going?"

"Nowhere special. Probably the library for a while."

"The keys are in my purse. I'm not going anywhere."

Judging by the sad look in her eyes and the full jug of wine next to the couch, I knew it was true.

There was only one thing I wanted to do—go to the Slosh and pour my heart out to Ruby. She would have some good advice for how to handle Aria. Even Oscar could be helpful in such a situation, I decided. Not because he was experienced with women—he wasn't—but because my life was beginning to resemble one of those Sci-Fi books he loved so much. Also, the Tortura boys would never look for me there, which was another plus. I didn't want to completely lie to my mother, either, so my first stop was the library. It was empty because of the upcoming holiday, which meant I had my pick of the computers. The first thing I did was Google Aria and see if I could find any pictures of her. There were some on Facebook, but I couldn't see them because I didn't have an account and wasn't "friends" with her. Then I looked up the news accounts of Mrs. Shanley's death.

It was pretty much like my mom said: she had disappeared, foul play was suspected but nothing was ever proven. One interesting thing I gathered from reading the accounts was that the local police force had taken a public relations black eye for their handling of the case. I didn't know enough about the technical aspects of the case to have an opinion, but I never understood why local cops were supposed to suddenly become brilliant detectives when something truly strange or extraordinary happened.

I did some more research on Mr. Shanley but nothing interesting came up, either online or in the news archives. There were a couple of mentions about his annual holiday bash in a few gossip columns and society magazines, but it didn't seem to rank that high on the social circuit. His financial company was so exclusive that they didn't even have a website. Then I sat in one of the big comfortable chairs in the main reading room and flipped through magazines, killing time. At quarter to seven there was an announcement over the intercom that the library would be closing in fifteen minutes, so I wrapped it up and headed to the Slosh.

Ruby and Oscar were the only two in the bar. Even the losers who hung out at the Slosh had better things to do around a holiday than go there. Ruby almost jumped when she saw me.

"Bert! What are you doing here?"

I grinned. "I live here, don't I?"

Even though the place was empty, Ruby leaned far over the bar before speaking again, giving me a killer view of those marshmallow fields I had chased Jesus through the other day. "The police were here. They were asking about you."

I took a deep breath and tried to stay calm. If so, it might even be a good thing. I would fight that rap with everything I could, and tell the cops about Carrot Top, and the golf club, everything. Maybe the Torturas had called the cops after all. Or maybe Carrot Top had decided to push his luck and report me for attempted assault, or for stealing a golf club that he had stolen from a potential murder scene. It didn't seem like I had too much to worry about. I took my stool and Ruby placed an open bottle mechanically in front of me, searching my face with her eyes, waiting for me to speak.

"What did they want?"

"You really don't know?"

"Of course not. That's why I'm asking."

"Remember that guy who was in here the other day, the one who hit you with the pool stick?"

"Of course. He and I have had several run-ins since then."

"You have?" Ruby's dark expression unnerved me.

"Yes," I continued, wanting to reassure her. "But it's all right, really. I've taken care of him, he won't be bothering me or anyone else for that matter anymore." I took a swig and smiled. "What about him?"

"He was murdered last night in Queens."

"MY GOD," Oscar screamed. "BERT, WHAT HAVE YOU DONE?"

I was like

I told Ruby and Oscar the story several times. Each time I stressed the fact that Carrot Top was very much alive and, except for some gingivitis, in good health when I last saw him. I knew they believed me, but they also knew enough about my earlier trouble with the law to recognize the similarities, of me going crazy and taking vigilante justice against a dirt bag. This had my m.o. all over it. Then they had a disagreement about the cause of death, which the detectives had not disclosed: Ruby said that this Marcus Rogers—which apparently was Carrot Top's real name— might have had a heart attack after I left. Oscar disagreed, and held the opinion that the fall out of the van must have caused a head trauma that killed him later. I told them it was not helping, and they stopped speculating.

It didn't change the facts: first, even if I wasn't responsible, the police still thought I was; and, second, if Carrot Top's death *was* directly related to our confrontation, then I had graduated from aggravated assault to full-blown homicide. And nothing I could say about Corky Healey, golf clubs, or ugly old clothing was going to save me. I wouldn't stand a chance. I suddenly missed those innocent, carefree days when all I had to worry about was the Tortura boys stomping a mud hole in my ass.

I stayed at the Slosh in a state of shock, staring into space, my eyes occasionally filling with tears, which I would discreetly wipe away before they could fall. Ruby and Oscar kept their distance, though Ruby would pat my hand sometimes and tell me everything was going to be all right. It was a nice lie, but it was still a lie. I thought about getting really drunk, but even the beer tasted bad to me.

I drank a couple over a few hours, very slowly, until they were warm and flat. I was numb, in a fog. A few customers came and went, but the place was mostly dead. I pushed away from the bar, threw down way too much cash, and walked out. I heard Ruby calling my name as I left. I ignored her.

As I slowed to turn into my mother's driveway, I saw an unfamiliar car parked in the space. Because of the angle I couldn't see far into the living room windows, but what I could see confirmed my suspicions. Two frowning men wearing ties were asking questions and taking notes. My mom has not been a big fan of the cops ever since my trial—even though it wasn't their fault, and they weren't the ones who charged me—but I also knew that if she had a few drinks in her, which was likely, they'd be able to get anything out of her. I could imagine the conversation they were having:

-*When did you last see your son, Mrs. Shambles?*

-A few hours ago. He spent the night.

-*What time did he come over?*

-I don't know. It was very late, after I was already asleep.

-*He let himself in with a key, I take it?*

-No, he used a ladder to climb in through his bedroom window.

-*Did you say a ladder?*

-That's right. Any law against a boy using a ladder to see his mom?

-*No, of course not. And how did he seem this morning?*

-Fine, except for some scratches on his face and arms, and the fact that he was missing a shoe...

Oh, it was a lovely conversation they were having.

I was suddenly gripped by a panic attack, deeper and more powerful than any I could remember: memories of the arrest, handcuffs, cops, lawyers, judges. Facing the Tortura boys would be better. I stepped on the gas and drove away as fast as I could.

It was pointless to run, and I knew it, but before I gave myself in and watched my whole life go back down the drain, permanently, there was one thing I had to do. A fool's errand. The only kind I know.

I drove down to the gas station on Shore Road, which had a working payphone on the side of the building. I dialed information, then used my last change to make the call.

A minute later I was back in my mom's car and heading across town, to a humble little subdivision bordering on the site of the former Mumfrey dump—a place that was still the subject of rumors about poisoned groundwater, increased birth defects, higher cancer rates, and other health problems for the people who lived nearby. Those concerns had long ago been silenced by the most powerful Long Island mob of all, the real estate mafia, and now any shoebox would sell for half a million whether there were two-headed dogs running around the yard or not.

I rang the bell and the front light went on, then the door opened.

"Well hello, stranger. If I'd known you were going to call I would have baked a cake."

It was a modest bungalow, tastefully decorated. There was music everywhere, a piano and keyboard, music stands, and posters advertising various jazz festivals and classical concerts. Scotty offered me the couch.

"Want something to drink?"

"Water would be great, thanks."

"Coming right up."

A minute later, Scotty returned and handed me a cold glass that had musical notes on it. I didn't care if it was poisoned groundwater or not. I gulped it down in a few glugs while he watched from an armchair.

"Are you all right? You sounded upset on the phone, and you don't look very good."

"I need a huge favor. I need you to make a phone call for me."

"You came all the way over here to use the phone?"

"No, I need you to make the call."

"Did you screw things up with Aria already?"

"Sort of. But I can't tell you any more, not yet. I just need you to say exactly what I tell you to say, and don't ask any questions for now. Is that okay?"

"Oh, Bert, Bert, Bert," he sighed sadly as he picked up the handset. "Okay, what's her number?"

"I was hoping you had it."

"As a matter of fact, I do." He flipped through an address book on the telephone table. "Here it is."

He dialed, then repeated what I had told him to say. When he hung up he was giving me a look.

"I think she'll be there," he said. "But I'm not happy about telling her it was a matter of life or death. Laying it on a little thick, don't you think?"

"It's not as far-fetched as it sounds," I said.

"I must tell you, Bert, speaking as a gay man, that in all my life I have never met a bigger drama queen than you."

Down near the end of Parsons Cove Road there's a poorly-marked turn that takes you down a nondescript little country lane, over a couple of quaint stone bridges, and up to the guard house of the Pondington Preserve. It was formerly the estate of a railroad tycoon, which he eventually donated to the town as a park. The place sits on five hundred acres of idyllic waterfront property high above Mumfrey Bay, with several miles of nature trails, babbling brooks, and a few hundred yards of rustic shoreline for the public to wander and enjoy. I worked there for a couple of summers in high school, clearing trails and maintaining the grounds. It's still my favorite place in Mumfrey. There are a few events over the summer that draw big crowds, but otherwise it's almost completely empty. I go there as often as I can.

I was a few minutes early. I pulled up to the gate and saw Charles working the security desk. I met Charles when I worked at the preserve and we had remained friends. He lets me go down to the beach at night, long after the park is closed. Back in high school it was the perfect place to bring girls, a guitar, and a few six-packs; whether it was a good place to meet a mobster's daughter while being the object of a manhunt for murder was yet to be seen. My Kumbaya-around-the-campfire days were long gone, probably forever, but I was glad Charles was still there.

It wasn't until I saw him, in his blue polyester uniform of shorts and short sleeve shirt, cheap badge, radio, work boots and tube socks, with his comfortingly familiar short blond hair and full beard, sitting behind his desk and working intently in his sketchbook, that I felt an intense wave of nostalgia wash over me. I suddenly missed those innocent days when I worked there and had a good county job that I could have held onto for twenty or thirty years, then retired with a pension while I was still young enough to enjoy it. He came outside, squinted at the car, recognized me and smiled. He reached into the window and gave my hand a firm squeeze. Charles was only a year or two older than me, but he seemed so much more mature and together.

"Bert! How you doing, buddy?"

"I'm good, Charles. Nice to see you."

"Going down to the beach? Hold on, I'll get the gate."

"Actually, I'm waiting for someone."

He grinned. "Say no more. Why don't you pull into the lot and let's hang out in the air conditioning."

I said it sounded great. I parked and went into the guard house. Charles was back at his desk, drawing in an oversized sketchbook and listening to a *Yes* album. "I've Seen All Good People" was just starting. Great song. I looked over his shoulder.

"What are you working on?"

"My costume for the Renaissance Festival. You should come. The storming of the castle is going to be awesome this year."

Charles lived in a fantasy world, mostly of his own making: dragons and wizards, princesses and goblins, *Dungeons and Dragons*, *Lord Of The Rings*: you name it, and he probably had the action figure for it. The highlight of his year was the Renaissance Festival. He was in his glory at those things. I went a couple of times, when I was working at the preserve. Charles did his rounds in tights and a harlequin outfit, with his security badge fastened to a breastplate and his walkie-talkie hanging next to a broadsword. I think he won the mutton-eating contest one year.

"I haven't seen you since last summer," he said finally, looking up from his notebook. "I think you were living in the city. How's it going?"

"I'm back now. Things didn't work out as I hoped."

"Sorry to hear that."

I didn't want to dump my troubles on Charles. He looked so happy there, sketching his checkered tights, breastplates, and helmet designs while *Yes* played. He was a gentle, friendly soul—the sort of person I wished I was. My problems seemed ugly by comparison.

Charles put down the pen and examined his work. "Not bad. Better let it dry. I'm going out for a smoke. Want to join me?"

"Sure."

We stood outside the guard house, filling the warm summer air with the beautiful smell of burning tobacco. I looked up at the blanket of stars and listened to the sounds of the woods, the crickets cricking and the raccoons pooping. I've always preferred the city to the country, but at that moment I appreciated the peace and solitude of nature more than ever. Maybe all of our problems just come from not knowing our place, not focusing on what's important. Charles had his sketchbook and progressive rock; what did I have?

"Someone's coming. This might be your friend."

A pair of headlights beamed from faraway down the long, narrow driveway. A minute later a late-model Chrysler pulled up, with Aria driving. I waved her into the lot behind the guard house. She was wearing tight jeans, white tennis shoes, and a skin-tight black AC/DC T-shirt. Charles took one look at her and the cigarette fell out of his mouth.

"By the blood of Zeus."

"Steady, Aragorn."

Aria had a hard expression on her face. She acted like Charles wasn't there.

"Okay, I'm here. Scotty said it was an emergency. What's going on?"

"Aria, this is Charles, the night security guard."

"Nice to meet you, Aria."

Charles extended a hand, which went unanswered until he withdrew it, sheepishly. He crushed out his cigarette.

"Excuse me, folks, I'll be heading back inside. Bert, just remember: my shift ends at midnight, so you guys will have to clear out before my replacement comes. Try to be back no later than a quarter to twelve."

He went back into the guard house.

"What is this place?"

"You've never been here?"

"I've passed it a million times, but never driven down here."

"Come on, I'll show you around."

"No. I don't want a tour, I want to know what was so important that you had Scotty do your dirty work for you."

"Would you have listened if I had called?"

"Of course not."

"That's why. But I can't explain it to you here. We'll talk down at the beach. It's just a short drive. I'll take you."

"If this is some kind of cheap ploy to try getting in my pants again, I swear I'm going to kill you myself with my bare hands."

"Don't you think I know that? It's not that; it's serious. Just get in the car. Please."

The layout of the preserve is impressive: beyond the guard house there are a few hundred feet of trees, then the road opens out onto a huge sloping field, with the two main castles on either side. It's very dramatic. The first castle, which was originally the carriage house and servants' quarters, is on the right. It's made up of two long, three-story stone wings with a huge turret in the middle that looks sort of like a hinge. The main house sits diagonally across the property and overlooks Long Island Sound. In the darkness I could see just the big, hulking outline of it.

As we passed the first castle, I could hear Aria catch her breath. She quickly recovered her steely composure. "Start talking."

"All right, look. I have to tell you something, and I wanted you to hear it from me before you heard it from someone else, so you could get my side of the story."

"I can't wait," she said, then yawned in such a way that I didn't think she meant it.

"I'm going to be arrested soon."

She twirled a finger. "Big whoop. I'm not surprised. What are you wanted for, murder?"

"Actually, yes."

Aria screamed so loudly that I almost went off the road into the bushes. I pulled the wheel hard and barely kept the car on the pavement. "I told you we should wait to talk!" I snapped.

She shoved my shoulder. "*Murder?* Is this some kind of joke? You think that's funny?"

"I wish. Remember that guy who broke into my room the other day?"

"How could I forget? He almost teed off on my freaking cranium."

"He was killed last night in Queens."

"And you didn't do it?"

"No."

"Then why would the police think you did?"

"Because I happened to be there around the same time."

"I see. Sort of like how my sister's empty wedding purse happened to be in your room?"

"I knew you wouldn't understand."

"Then why are you trying to explain it to me?"

"Because I wanted to tell you why I didn't show up last night. I was on my way, but stopped to see if Mrs. Healey was all right first. He was just leaving the house when I got there, so I followed him and we had a confrontation somewhere in Astoria. But I ran off and never touched the guy. He had the bags of clothes and Corky Healey's missing putter in the van."

"What was he doing with those?"

"I don't know exactly. We were interrupted before he could tell me everything. He said he was looking for something in one of the pockets, something valuable that Corky had promised him."

"What was he looking for?"

"I don't know. I couldn't find out in time."

"Before you killed him?"

"No, before some nosy old guy interrupted us. I ran off. I never laid a hand on him."

"Then how do you know you're a suspect?"

"Cops came by the bar I hang out at, looking for me. They told the bartender and she told me."

"Oh."

"Yeah."

"Then why are you telling me all this? Sounds like you should be talking to a lawyer instead."

"I'll tell you, but this time you have to wait until the car is parked."

We drove the rest of the way in silence, down to where the road dead-ends at a sandy little lot near the beach. There was a beautiful half-moon in the sky. It was warm but a steady breeze kept it from being oppressive, and the gentle waves made tiny splashing noises on the beach.

"Start talking."

I told her everything as we walked, starting from when Aria left the rooming-house to when I saw the detectives at my mom's house. When I was done she stopped and looked at me.

"Okay, now I know the story. But that still doesn't explain why you had Scotty pressure me to meet you." Her tone was still hard and unforgiving, but I felt like there was a slight thaw beginning to creep into her tone. I had to take what I could get.

"I know you don't think very much of me, Aria, and I don't blame you. But I wanted you to know that I really *was* on my way over to your house when this happened, and that I had nothing to do with any murder except for the fact that I almost died laughing, seeing the expression on the guy's face when I left him on the ground, crying. And as for your sister's money, I didn't steal that either. There's no amount of money that could be worth losing a girl like you over, corny as it sounds. Your parents can hate me and your brothers can beat the crap out of me, but I would still be grateful for every moment we've spent together. That's all I wanted to say, and why I had Scotty call."

"So, with all this going on, that's what you were most concerned about? Telling me how you feel about me?"

"Yes. Pretty pathetic, I know."

Aria considered this, looking out over the water. Then she buried her face in her hands and started to cry.

"It's not pathetic, it's beautiful. Nobody has ever spoken to me like that before. I'm so sorry, Bert. I'm sorry for everything."

"Why are you sorry? I got myself into this mess."

"You don't understand." She took a deep breath. "I know you didn't steal that money."

"You're just saying that because you feel sorry for me."

"No, I'm saying it because *I* stole the money."

What

"It wasn't something I planned, I just did it impulsively. My sister is a horrible human being and I can't stand her, and I wanted to teach her a lesson."

"When did you have the time? I was with you on the beach."

"Right before I came downstairs, to watch you turn pages while Scotty was playing. My fat cow of a sister was so drunk she left the purse in a bathroom. Nobody saw me go in or come out. It took about ten seconds, and by the time she realized what she had done I was long gone."

"So why did you put the empty purse in my car? To frame me?"

"No! I swear, I had no idea it was your car. It just looked like some old, nasty car one of my dumb uncles would drive."

"That car happens to be a classic."

"Sorry. The point is, I hid the money in a vent where I sometimes hide cigarettes or other things I don't want my prying parents to find. I don't know what I was thinking. At first I just wanted to take some of the money, as payment for what a jerk she's been to me over the years. Her husband was interested in me at first, but when she found out how rich he is she went after him really aggressively."

"Why would he choose her over you? No offense, but your sister's a cow."

"I know! That makes it even more humiliating." She sniffled, then laughed sadly. "How else do you think it happened? Sex. I wanted to wait for my wedding night, but she doesn't have the same values. She has a mouth like a sump pump, and that scrambles a lot of guys' brains, or what passes for brains in most men. She told him that I was frigid, controlling, some kind of ice princess who was only going to toy with him before breaking his heart. But nothing could be further from the truth; I just wanted to make it special. And now he's stuck with that fat, evil bitch and I hope he regrets it every day for the rest of his life."

"So you took the purse to teach her a lesson. What happened?"

"I was going to put some money in my secret hiding place, but before I knew it I had emptied the whole thing. Then I thought I heard someone coming upstairs, and there wasn't enough room to fit the purse too, so I had to sneak it outside, to make people think the culprit must have run off. Your car was right there, except I didn't know it was yours so I just dropped it in the open window. You really should lock your car up, you know."

"So my astrologer tells me. But you've really messed up my life as a result."

"I know! I'm sorry. When I found the purse in your room I realized what had happened, and the stupid mistake I had made. I knew it was God's way of punishing me. I finally met a nice boy, someone who was different from the clowns my family keeps trying to set me up with, and I ruined everything, for both of us."

"So why didn't you tell me, instead of freaking out at my place?"

"I was scared! I was planning on losing my virginity to you, which I was excited about but also nervous. Then that crazy guy came in and almost killed both of us. Then, just as things were turning nice again I found the purse. It seemed like no matter where I turned there was someone or something telling me that I was a bad person, and about to make an even bigger mistake. Then I was mad at you for not telling that you had the purse. I thought maybe you were trying to trick me or something. But my heart was breaking the whole time, knowing that I was lying to you."

"If that's how you felt, then why did you send your brothers after me?"

"I didn't! That's the crazy thing. When you didn't show up last night I was upset, of course. I tried not to show it but my mom could tell something was wrong. Long story short, all I said was that we had plans for that evening but that something must have come up because you didn't show up or call. Well, my mom said something to my brothers, and they took it as an insult, so they wanted to teach you a lesson. By that time I was already in bed, asleep. Otherwise I never would have allowed it. I freaked when I found out."

"Let me get this straight. First your brothers wanted to beat me up for spending time with you, now they want to beat me up for *not* spending time with you?"

"You're starting to understand my family."

We had gone around to the far side of the inlet, way beyond the property line of the preserve. I was very tired again. I had forgotten how potentially life-threatening and exhausting relationships were. "We should be heading back," I said.

Aria was scanning the sandy cliff that led up from the beach. She looked left, then right, then stepped back and looked again. "It's just up the hill there."

"What is?"

She scrambled to the top of the sandy cliff and disappeared into the overgrowth. I felt very alone on that rocky little beach, so I climbed up after her. I found her at the edge of a big stretch of grass, looking into the distance.

"What is it?"

"This is the back of the Pondington Country Club. Come on, follow me." She walked diagonally across the grass.

"A little late for a game of croquet, don't you think?"

"I'm not fooling around. It's just over here."

"What is?"

"The Healey house."

"Why are we going to the Healey's?"

"Because I want to know what the hell is going on! We're going to sit down with Mrs. Healey and have a nice little chat, about Bill Shanley, and this dead guy, and her husband."

"Aren't we trespassing?"

She dismissed my concern with a wave. "I'm a member."

We were sheltered by a line of trees and thick hedges running along the edge of the property After a few hundred feet, Aria stopped and peered through an opening in the bushes.

"This is it. We used to play Night Patrol and tag around here when I was a kid. The Healey kid—Dale—was sort of friendly with my brother Marco for a while."

We came out on the edge of the Healey property. The house looked much more impressive from the rear. It had been cut into the hill in such a way that from the front it looked like a humble flagstone ranch, but from the rear of the yard it was a sprawling, multi-level thing. I crouched on one knee and looked for a way to the house, using the trees and shrubbery as cover. Aria walked straight across the lawn like she owned the place.

"Serpentine!" I hissed.

She turned and motioned impatiently. "Come *on*."

I crouched alongside her. "You trying to get me into even more trouble?"

"For what? Ringing a woman's doorbell to see if she's all right? Besides, I told you, I know the Healeys. Not very well, but they certainly know my family."

Well, that was that. I was heartened by her confidence, but I also thought her bravado was easy, considering she wasn't facing life in prison for murder. I decided to try it her way. I straightened up and walked tall and proud, swinging my arms. "Lovely night for a stroll, don't you think?"

"You don't have to overdo it."

"What if she's asleep?"

"Then I'm waking her sleepy ass up, aren't I?"

We went to the front of the house. Aria knocked and rang, then peered through the frosted windows.

"See anything?"

"Nope. She's probably down at the clubhouse, doing last-minute stuff for the fundraiser."

"What if she's dead?"

"I doubt it. She's one of the main people on the committee. People would be wondering where she was."

"Let's go," I said. "It's hopeless. I'll turn myself in tomorrow, if I'm not picked up before then."

"Let's go down to the clubhouse and see if she's there."

"And have a big drama in front of the Ladies' Auxiliary Steering Committee for the Placement of Bunting? Not a chance."

Aria looked ready to spit. "This sucks. This really, really stinks."

We started back the way we came, across the lawn. Halfway to the property line I paused. "Unless—"

"Unless what?"

"Nothing. Dumb idea. Forget it."

"Tell me."

"I just remembered something. When I was here a few days ago, picking up the clothes for the church, I happened to see the code that Dale punched in for the garage door." I snorted. "Told you it was dumb."

Aria's eyes widened. "Really? Why the hell didn't you say so? Let's go."

She marched back to the house. I followed behind, protesting the whole time that it was foolish, but also not caring anymore. Anything that allowed me to spend more time with her was a good thing. We got to the garage doors and I found the keypad.

"This is crazy."

"Why? We have a perfectly valid reason for going in."

"Such as?"

"Our concern over a poor widow who might have been the victim of a crime. You can wait out here if you're too scared, but give me the code."

I sighed and punched in 2-1-1-2. Somewhere inside a motor began to whirr, and I could hear the opening chords of "The Temple of Syrinx" start to play in my head. The left garage door began sliding open. Aria was pleased, and flashed me a broad grin.

"Pretty slick. You think like a thief, as my father would say. He means it as a compliment."

"I'm sure."

"I'll only be a minute. You hide out of sight until I come back."

"No. I'm coming too."

"Are you sure? I can probably tell what a dead body looks like."

"No, not that. I want to look for something else."

"Like what?"

"Like, a reason why some bags of ugly old clothes are worth drying for."

"You mean dying."

"What did I say?"

"Drying."

"Just a typo. I'll go first."

We were on the lowest level of the house. The door from the garage led into a corridor with several other rooms coming off it, including a laundry room. The rest were mainly storage. There was a door at the end of the corridor, and beyond that a large, open game room, with windows looking out over the yard toward the golf course.

Rows of trophies lined the walls, and there was a big tent-like device with a screen that Aria told me was a golfing simulator. The trophies were mostly for golf, but there were others, for skiing and skeet-shooting and a ladies' amateur golf league, that had Dorothy's name on them. She had been quite an athlete too, which explained her firm grip and slim, youthful, attractive appearance.

It was the type of room I dreamed of as a kid. There was a pinball machine, half-court basketball, weight-lifting and workout devices, dart boards and shuffleboard and a large, ornate pool table in the middle. I always enjoyed playing pool, but every time I saw a table now I shuddered, after taking that beating from Carrot Top, or Marcus Rogers, or whatever his name was.

Aria went over to the pool table and crouched over it, holding an imaginary pool stick in her hand and pretending to shoot.

"Eight ball, corner pocket."

Her right hand drew back and shot forward at the imaginary ball. "This is a nice table," she said appreciatively.

"Quit fooling around," I snapped.

She put on a face. "Why can't I have a little fun? This is exciting. I've never done anything like this before."

"Let's look upstairs."

We went up the open staircase at the rear of the game room until we were on the main level. At the top was a huge family room. The kitchen was off to one side, and ahead of us was the main hallway through the rest of the house. Aria found a dimmer switch and put the lights in the family room on low. The place looked like a furniture showroom, mostly white and curvy pieces. Aria stretched out on one of the sofas.

"These people have nice taste. It's so different from my house. I feel like I can relax here. I could curl up and sleep for a while."

She took a silver frame off the side table.

"Is this Mrs. Healey when she was younger? God, she was stunning."

She turned the frame around so I could see. It was another shot of Corky and Dorothy, posing on a beach somewhere sunny and nice and a boy who I assumed was little Dale, at only ten years old or so. Corky had the same squint and cocky grin. He had fair reddish-blond hair and a rugged, tan face, his strong forearms dusted with freckles and sun-bleached hair. Dorothy was a natural blonde, radiant and beautiful in a white bikini.

The picture flipped down. Aria frowned at me.

"That's enough drooling over the hot babe." She put the picture back on the table, stretched again and yawned.

"Listen, Bert, it's time to make a decision. If you're looking for something, let's look for it. Just give me a clue. We have to be back before midnight or your friend said we're going to turn into pumpkins."

"What time is it now?"

She looked at her watch. "Eleven-twenty."

"The best thing to look for would be some kind of date book or diary, or maybe a phone book. There's an office up in front of the house. I'll check there. You check these rooms. And be sure not to put too many lights on, and leave everything exactly as it was."

"Aye-aye, Captain."

I found the front office, turned on the small desk lamp and poked around the desk. Things were very neatly arranged: bills, unopened mail, nothing unusual. Ditto in the drawers.

There was a flash of light in the room. I crouched behind the desk chair. Through the sheer curtains that faced the front of the house I could see a car pulling into the driveway. It kept going around the semi-circle and disappeared down to the side, the garage. I ran back down the corridor. Aria was at a little work area off to the side of the kitchen, a telephone hutch and desk that was much messier.

"Bert, I was looking through—"

I took her by the arm. "No time. Someone's here."

We ran back downstairs to the game room. We got to the sliding glass doors. Aria slid one panel open and slipped into the dark of the backyard patio just as someone came into the game room.

I pulled Aria to the side and we waited. It was Dale Healey. He was rolling a bag behind him. I took one step across the patio and must have triggered a motion sensor, because two brilliant, blazing floodlights turned the patio into midday. We hauled ass out of there. We didn't stop until we were back on the far side of the golf course.

"Think he saw us?"

"Not sure. Possible."

"That was fun."

"I'm glad one of us thinks so."

Aria was holding an envelope in her hands.

"What's that?"

"I'm not sure. I was looking through it when you grabbed me. Some kind of vacation brochures, for a resort or something. Maybe she went on a trip somewhere."

"We'll deal with that later. How are we doing on time?"

"We can make it."

We hustled back to the preserve, where we found Charles reclining on the sea wall, smoking a joint.

"How was it, guys?" He had a great grin.

"Did we make it back in time?"

"The overnight guard called. He's running late. He won't be here for another hour at least. Wanna smoke a doob?"

"You get high at work?" Aria was stunned. "Don't you have to pass a drug test or something?"

"Lady, this is a county job. I buy my weed from my boss."

"Maybe next time," I said. "We'd better be going."

"Suit yourself. Just be sure to close the gate."

"Will do."

As we walked away, Aria said, "Maybe I should get a job like that. Seems like a pretty sweet gig." I grunted and smiled. Charles was a great guy and all, but he was still dreaming of fair maidens, while I left with one. I drove Aria back to her car. We both pulled through the gate then I got out and closed it. I walked over to her car, and she got out, looking up expectantly at me. "What now?"

"What else? I'll go back to my mom's house, where I will either get arrested on the spot or else first thing in the morning."

"And you're okay with that? You can just accept it like it's no big deal?"

"Of course it's a big deal! What do you want me to do, go on the lam? I have no power, no money, no alibi, no defense. I've got nothing. I'm dead meat."

"You're forgetting something."

"What?"

Aria took my hand.

"You've got me."

So

I know what you're thinking. I was thinking it too, the whole drive over to her house. Fantasies of capping off my last night of freedom with tears and tenderness and some hot, weepy sex. We had made up from our fight, taken a moonlit walk on the beach, and broken into a stranger's house. It was the most romantic evening I had ever had.

It wasn't until we got to the Tortura driveway that I got paranoid and wondered if I was being set up. My heart started racing and my palms began to sweat. Aria parked in the big circular gravel driveway and I pulled up behind her but left the engine running. She came over and looked in.

"What's wrong?"

"Where's your family?"

"I told you. They're out on the boat for a few days. Nobody is home, trust me."

I got out and followed her into a side entrance that led into a landing and some back stairs, up to the second floor. As I followed her up the stairs in silence I got a sudden, terrible sense of her loneliness. Aria showed me to a guest room and I peeled out of my clothes in about ten wobbly seconds and then I was under the covers and passed out.

In the morning I had no idea where I was. I scrambled to my feet, looked around, blinked, then sat back down. I heard doors opening and closing so I jumped back under the covers and peeked out through a slit in my eyelids as Aria opened the door quietly and looked in on me. She was wearing a bathrobe and dragging a comb through her hair. She walked gently over to the bed, leaned over, and kissed me softly on the lips. She smelled like steam and soap, cherry lip gloss and the Easter bunny. I opened my eyes.

"Good morning. Did you sleep well?"

"Do that again and I'll tell you."

She kissed me harder. I'd never felt a pair of lips like that. Not that I'm the most experienced guy in the world, but still. She made some soft noises, and lifted one leg up onto the bed and lay partly on top of me, and moved back and forth slowly so I could get the full effect of her small, warm body. She pushed herself up and smiled.

"I can see that there's one part of you that has no trouble getting up in the morning."

Torture. She lived up to her name. But I also knew that the time for joking was over. I thought about what lay ahead of me, the handcuffs and fingerprinting and interrogations, and I choked up.

"What's wrong?"

I shook my head, unable to answer and the tears slid out of the sides of my eyes and wet my ears. Aria's smile dropped and she searched my face. She didn't move, just stayed propped up, looking at me with a curious expression I hadn't seen before. It was almost like something had sprung loose or broken free, something good but maybe a little crazy too, and then she was on me for real, kissing me with a force and passion I hadn't felt since the early days with Devil Girl, and then her robe fell to the floor and the covers parted and it happened.

It happened.

IT. HAPPENED.

There are some things I just can't talk about. Some things are still sacred to me. The funny thing was that this time I was the one who tried to stop it. I told her to be very sure, and careful, and she said it would be all right and that she wanted to, needed to, that I had awakened something in her, some kind of freedom or courage, and that she had messed my life up enough as it was with the wedding purse and her crazy brothers and all the rest, and that she had never been so sure of anything.

It didn't last very long, and I was as gentle and considerate as I could be, but it was also clear to me that this was a moment she had thought about many times, long before I came into her life, so there was a sureness, a confidence behind the awkwardness that allowed her to be in control even though it was her first time. We kissed and cried, and when it was over we laughed as she snuggled close. After a few drowsy minutes she came back to reality.

"I don't want you to think I'm pulling away from you, because I'd love nothing more than to stay in your arms, but we've still got a pretty serious day ahead."

"It's all settled," I said. "I know what' going to do. I can face anything after that."

She got out of bed and put her robe on. "Don't run off just yet. I have some ideas. We can talk them over at breakfast. There are fresh towels and a robe in the bathroom, and there should be a new toothbrush in the drawer by the sink."

Aria kissed me and was gone. I lay there for a few minutes, eyes closed, taking in her scent and replaying the last half hour. I finally got up to use the bathroom. The bathroom was huge, much bigger than my room, and was decked out with gold-plated fixtures, multiple lighting and heating controls, and a giant whirlpool tub that was separate from the shower. And of course marble, plenty, in several different colors. I took a long, hot shower and scrubbed myself with all the fancy extracts, botanicals, oils and masques that were lined up on the shelf. I came out smelling sweet and minty fresh. My fellow inmates would love that.

I dried off, brushed my teeth and put on the robe. I went back into the bedroom to get dressed but my clothes were gone. I went downstairs and found the kitchen. Aria was busy with a bunch of bowls and ingredients. She smiled shyly when she saw me come in, and I went behind her and wrapped my arms around her waist. She grabbed my forearms and squeezed them.

"Are you okay?"

"I think so." She turned around and we kissed. "How was your shower?"

"Great, but someone stole my clothes."

"I put them in the wash, smartass. Breakfast will be ready soon. Coffee's over there."

"Thanks."

I pulled the toothbrush from the pocket of the robe. "Can I keep this?"

"Of course." She pointed with the spatula, to a manila envelope on the huge marble island in the middle of the kitchen. The return address on the envelope was Shanley Investments, which I recognized as being located in a dreary office park down by the old sand pits. There were brochures inside, for some kind of vacation resort. On the front of the first brochure there was a yellow sticky note. It said *Dotty, What do you think? –B.*

"I don't get it," I said. "Is this important?"

"Think about it; I'm sure the answer will come to you. I have to get the muffins out of the oven."

I looked at the brochures again. They were filled with the standard sort of stock photos: perfect golf courses, horseback riding, fifty-something couples clicking wine glasses and looking wealthy and confident.

"I got it," I said. "Bill and Dorothy Healey are having an affair, and they're planning a vacation together."

Aria rolled her eyes as she placed the hot muffin pan on the stove. "Did you actually *read* anything in the brochures?"

"It's early. I haven't had my coffee yet."

I got a mug, filled it, then took the brochures over to a big round table by the windows and started reading. It was a vacation resort, yes, but one that hadn't been built yet. The brochures were sales materials for a national chain of golf-themed retirement communities. The place was going to be called Corky's Club. Inside the back flap, there was a logo, the center of which was a stately portrait of a smiling Corky Healey, giving his blessing to the venture from beyond the grave, the one he was probably doing somersaults in at that very moment. He looked like the Orville Redenbacher of cheesy geriatric theme parks.

I don't know anything about business or investing, but it looked like Shanley was hoping to cash in on the huge wave of retiring Baby Boomers in the coming years. The communities were centered around something called the Active Lifestyle Concept, which as far as I could tell was based on the idea that old people who did stuff would be happier than those who didn't, or something.

"What do you think?"

"I'm not sure. Mrs. Healey told me that Corky never did endorsements. So I doubt he would have agreed to lend his name to something like this. Maybe now that he's gone, they can finally go ahead."

"Or maybe they got rid of him because he wouldn't play along."

"Come on, that's crazy."

"Is it? It takes time to put stuff like this together. Corky's only been gone a few weeks, so Dorothy and Bill must have been planning this for a long time. At least a year, maybe longer. See what I'm saying?"

"I guess so."

"You're not convinced?"

"No, not at all. Using the guy's name for something like this might be insensitive, but is it really something to kill the old guy over?"

"Why not? If there's enough money involved, sure, I'll believe anything."

"And people say I'm paranoid."

"They do?"

"Yes, but only behind my back."

Aria thought about it for a moment, then her shoulders dropped. "I honestly don't know what to think. I guess it was too much to hope for, that I could find something important. I just wanted to believe I could help in some way."

"You have helped, a great deal. I'm not nearly as lonely or afraid as I was before."

She smiled slightly, then brought two plates around the kitchen island to the big table. "If you're not lonely or afraid, then I hope you're still hungry, at least."

It was another feast: eggs blended with chopped ham and chives and cream cheese, homemade hash browns, and warm sourdough rolls. There was enough coffee cake, muffins, croissants, yogurt and fruit for ten people. We sat on stools at one of the islands and ate in silence. I really wanted to have some great insight or breakthrough, but nothing occurred to me.

"I've got it," Aria said finally.

"What?"

"Listen. Bill and this Marcus guy were in cahoots. Marcus had the clothes and the club, and we saw them walking together on the beach, going on his boat. I know Bill is up to no good. We're going to nail him. We just have to make a plan, and we have to move quickly."

I smiled. Aria had not seen the same PBS mystery shows that I had. I cleared my throat.

"You don't understand; all we have is what is known in police lingo as *circumstantial* evidence. Without hard proof I'm afraid our investigation is over before it's begun." I took a bite of a steaming blueberry muffin to drive home the point. Aria narrowed her eyes again in that way that I was becoming unhappily familiar with, though at the same time it sent a thrill down my spine every time. She exhaled sharply, walked over to a drawer in the side of the island, opened it and removed an address book.

"What are you doing?"

She ignored me as she flipped through the pages, then ran her finger down a page. She picked up the phone and dialed, then folded her free arm under the one holding the phone and waited.

"Hello, is this Bill Shanley? Hi Bill, it's Aria Tortura. Fine thanks." She rolled her eyes as she said it. "Why am I calling? Funny you should ask. Here's the deal. A friend and I found what you and Marcus were looking for. We know everything. You either make a deal or we go to the cops." I heard a scream or yell from the other end; Aria winced as she pulled the receiver away from her ear, then she continued. "No, this is not a joke. We're deadly serious. What? My dad? Go ahead and call him. Who do you think he's going to believe, his youngest daughter or the middle-aged creep who hits on her every chance he gets?" Then she nodded and smiled slightly. "That's what I thought you'd say. Wait for our call if you know what's good for you. No, it's not a threat, this isn't blackmail. But you've caused some serious problems for my friend, that he didn't deserve, and you're going to set things straight or else you will have a big problem on your hands. Understand? That's what I thought you'd say."

She hung up. I stared at her with my mouth open.

"*That* was your big plan? To call Bill Shanley and just talk crazy to him?"

"You got any better ideas? I've got him about ready to crap his pants."

"Oh, really? That's wonderful, and I hope he does crap himself, but you're forgetting something."

"What?"

"We don't know what he was after, or what he's done, or anything."

Aria looked at me sadly and shook her head.

"Haven't you ever heard of bluffing?"

"Of course! But that's not bluffing, it's just b.s. What do we have? What if he calls our bluff?"

"You still have the golf club, don't you?"

"It was in my room. I have no idea if it's still there. Your brothers might have taken it, to beat me with. Or maybe the cops have already found it and now I'm going to be charged with Corky's murder on top of Marcus'."

"Take it easy, babe. We're not going to have to do anything with Bill. I have a feeling he's going to make the next move. The point of bluffing isn't just to trick the other person into believing something untrue, it's to scare them into making a mistake."

Some music started to play. Aria held up her phone and smiled. "Bingo. He's already hooked." She answered with a low, serious tone. "Hello? What? We don't want money, this isn't blackmail. Nice try. This is about you getting what you deserve. I told you the price. You're going to see to it that my friend doesn't have any more trouble from anyone about this. I don't care what it means. No, that time won't work, we've got some other calls to make. We've got multiple backups, and anything you do to mess with us will backfire. I told you, wait until you get our further instructions. Don't call again or the deal is off. And if you don't pick up your phone when I call, the deal is off. If you contact anyone else or try to pull a fast one, the deal is off." She clicked off the phone and put it on the counter. "God, what an asshole."

"Trying to trap you?"

"It was so transparent. He's all like, 'How much will it take, you don't understand, it's not what it looks like, blah blah blah.' Then he was asking what my friend's name was, and how could he arrange anything if he didn't know who I was talking about, like I'm really that stupid."

"Speaking of stupid, I have a question."

"What?"

"What do we do now?"

"First, we need to get that golf club from your place, if it's still there. That's our first stop."

I shook my head. "I can't go back to the rooming-house. What if the cops are there?"

"I hadn't thought of that." She drummed her fingers on the marble counter. "Okay, I'll go to the rooming-house and see if it's there."

"Fine," I said, helping myself to more eggs, "I'll wait here."

"No."

"No?"

"No. I have a better idea."

Aria picked the phone up again and started to dial. I had a sinking feeling that her idea of a better idea wasn't the same as mine.

After that

Half an hour later Aria and I were standing in front of her house, by the big fountain, sharing a cigarette. She scanned the road down below, at the end of the long driveway. I had pulled my car into one of the bays of the giant detached garage off one wing of the house that held several luxury cars, a few motorcycles, ATVs, and a trailer with two gleaming Wave Runners.

"Do you really think this is going to work?"

"I have no idea."

"I'm so screwed."

"Don't say that. We have to stay cool and in control."

"So while you're at the rooming-house looking for a putter that might not even be there, I'm supposed to just waltz into the Pondington Country Club and intimidate Bill Shanley?"

"That's right. We can't give him any more time to work up a defense, or get an alibi straight."

"So I should get my ass kicked by him instead?"

"Stop it. Nothing will happen to you. I told you, I know his type. The more aggressive and in control you pretend to be, the more he will respect you. That's what guys like Shanley responds to, a kind of brute, animal confidence."

"Are you sure we're talking about Shanley, or you?" Aria stubbed out the cigarette.

"Get serious, Bert, I know his type all too well. Besides, you didn't hear the fear in his voice. We've got him on the run. The best defense—"

"Is a good offense," I said. "I know. My concern is that we don't have any offense at all. You need to be in possession of the ball to play offense. Not only do we not have the ball, we don't know what it looks like or even where the field is."

"Thank you, Mister Optimism."

"You can't blame me for being a little short on confidence at this point."

"Trust me, Bert. We need to act like we're in charge, even if we're not."

A compact car made the turn and came through the open gate. The car pulled onto the gravel circle. The door opened and Scotty got out. He looked at us and grinned.

"Well, well. Last night you were in the dumps, Bert, and this morning you've already moved in. I'd say I'm quite a matchmaker."

Aria gave him a kiss and hug. "Thanks for coming."

"My pleasure, I was on my way to the club to start setting up soon anyway. I'll just set up a little earlier than I planned and eat more free food."

I slipped into the passenger side and slid down low in the seat. Aria came over and handed me her cellphone.

"You better hold onto this, you might need it."

"Thanks."

"And you have the other envelope?"

Aria and I had decided that whatever they were looking for, it was small enough to fit in a pocket, so she had found a plain white envelope and put one of the small Corky's Club brochures inside, then wrote PERSONAL AND CONFIDENTIAL on the front. I checked my back pocket. "I've got it," I said.

"Remember, that's only if Shanley demands some kind of proof. You can show it to him, but you have to make sure he doesn't get that envelope from you, or the whole thing falls apart. Also, don't let him talk business until I get there."

She stepped back from the car, arms crossed, a look of intense worry on her face. Scotty started up and the wheels began rolling on the gravel, crunching.

"Stop!"

Scotty slammed on the brakes. Even going that slow I almost smashed into the dashboard. I stopped myself just in time and turned to Aria. "What?!"

She didn't say anything. She ran over, leaned into the window, and kissed me. Then she stepped back and waved, tears in her eyes.

"Oh, the tragedy of young love," Scotty sighed, and we continued on our way. We reached Mumfrey Boulevard in silence before he spoke again.

"So I understand the first part of the plan. I try getting you into the club as my page-turner, like we did before, at the Tortura's."

"Right."

"Then what?"

"I'm not really sure. All I know is that the alternative is life at Rikers."

"Actually, I'm pretty sure they won't send you to Rikers Island. They'll probably send you to Leavenworth, or Sing-Sing, or one of those SuperMax prisons where you sit in a tiny, windowless cell for twenty-three hours a day."

"I hate you."

"Oh, don't be so serious, Bert, I'm just fooling around. How could you go to prison when you've done nothing wrong?"

"What planet are you living on?"

"I can see I've touched a nerve. Sorry."

"In the last few days I've been beaten up, almost choked to death, been chased by a gang of thugs—"

"What thugs?"

"Aria's brothers."

"Why? Because of the money?"

"No, because I didn't show up for a date."

Scotty tried to process this, failed, and shook his head. "Continue."

"—And now the guy who beat me up is dead and I'm wanted by the cops. I'm going to confront the guy who's behind all of this, and make sure it stops, which means I'll probably be beaten up and charged with a bunch of other crimes before the day it out."

"And I thought I had a busy social life. Look, Bert, all I can tell you is, if you've done nothing wrong then you've got nothing to fear. Yes, I know sometimes the wrong people get convicted for things, but not guys like you."

"You're wrong. Guys like me get shafted all the time, especially when they have no money, connections, power, or friends."

The wheel jerked and Scotty almost drove us off the road as he pulled over. He turned to me, a stern look on his face.

"Listen to me, Bert Shambles, you have plenty of friends. Your mom. Fr. Pete. Me. Aria." He paused. "Well, maybe that's not a lot, but that's more than some people have. So please spare me the pity party, mm-kay? I know you're scared, and I'm sorry I made light of it, but the point is to rely on the friends you *do* have, and stop complaining about the ones you don't."

I had never thought of it like that. I looked out the window rather than answer.

"Get out."

"What?"

"You heard me. Get out of the car."

I got out. Scotty opened his door, got out and walked around to my side. "You drive the rest of the way."

"Why?"

"Just do it, please."

I did as he asked. I was squashed up against the steering wheel. Scotty showed me how to adjust the seat. Soon we were moving again, with me driving.

"I still don't know what we're doing."

"You'll see. Make the next left."

I did as he instructed. Just ahead, a guard waited at the entrance gate to the Pondington Country Club. Scotty leaned over and handed the guard a large, stiff white card with raised gold lettering on it.

"Name please?"

"Scotty Murrow, the keyboardist for today's festivities."

The guard checked a list. "Okay." Then he held out his hand to me. "Invitation."

"This gentleman is my roadie."

"Your what?"

"He is here to unload and set up my equipment, then he is leaving. Union rules. Very strict. You may call the organizer, Mr. William Shanley, if you have any questions."

My jaw clenched a little at the mention of Shanley, which was a foolish bit of improvisation that Scotty added. The guard couldn't have cared less. He waved us in with a tired expression.

I nodded in the way I thought a roadie would, then rolled in slowly. Scotty was pleased. "My little ruse worked perfectly," he cackled.

"Nice work, 007."

There were some young guys in club shirts, acting as valets. I told one of them what we were there for and he directed us to an employee parking lot. We parked and unloaded the equipment.

"Give me a couple of minutes."

I walked back over to where a few of the young valets were sitting, under a big umbrella. They all looked tan, muscular, and clean-cut. One of them looked at me and I smiled at him.

"Can I help you, sir?"

"Maybe. I was wondering which car Bill Shanley drove in today. Does he have that sweet black Mercedes today?"

The young guy grinned. "You like that car, huh?"

"Six figures," one of the other young guys added. "They only import something like a hundred of them each year."

"This sounds really dumb, but could I take a look at it? I've only seen it from a distance."

The first valet hopped up. "Totally. I'll show you where it's parked."

"No test drives," the other guy joked.

We walked down the driveway to a side lot. It was a beast of a machine, low and angular and intimidating. I'm pretty proud of the Olds but this car could have given it an inferiority complex. I pretended to look carefully inside the driver's window.

"What do you think?"

"I think I need a better job," I laughed.

"You and me both," the valet said. I walked around to the back of the car. There was a white oval sticker with STK on it.

"That's all my poor heart can stand," I sighed. I reached into my pocket.

"There's really no need for that, sir," he said. I nodded once then shook his hand and walked back to where Scotty was waiting. "In the market for a new car?"

"Something like that."

We got the gear, then went in through the employee entrance. From there we were directed to a hospitality desk upstairs, on the main level, where Scotty once again showed his invitation and explained that I was his assistant. The ladies gave us badges to wear. Official-looking ladies wearing special ribbons and carrying clipboards hurried here and there; one of them zeroed in on us and, after consulting her clipboard, asked us to follow her.

The main clubhouse looked like something from *Gone With The Wind.* Big white pillars, a huge porch, and lots of stately rooms filled with oil paintings and sculptures, pianos and leather furniture, high ceilings and crystal chandeliers. There were wood-paneled club rooms and reading rooms lined with bookshelves, dining rooms, trophy rooms, barrooms, and tasteful signs pointing the way to the pool, workout rooms, game areas, and of course the pro shop. I scanned the rooms and the faces of people as we passed but didn't see Dorothy Healey or Bill Shanley.

We were led out to the rear patio, which had a matching set of giant pillars and wide steps leading down a large, rolling lawn that opened onto the golf course beyond. I could see more people out on the course, coming and going, either taking part of the tournament or else spectating.

We were taken to a corner of the patio to set up in, near one of the bar stations. As we unpacked I thought about two concepts that Dr. K. had talked about, having and belonging. How we all tend to define ourselves by either what we have or what we're part of. Dr. K. felt that that a lot of my problems came from not knowing my father— where he is or even if he's alive. I'm willing to believe that, but then what was everybody else's excuse? Because as far as I could see, country clubs were all about having and belonging: you had to have enough money to join, and then be accepted as someone worthy of belonging. As far as I could tell, the only thing tying these people together was the fact that they could afford to join and had been accepted. And they were all white, of course. Islands within islands. I didn't understand how it all worked and doubted that I ever would.

We put down the equipment and I looked around. Scotty pulled a few wires out of a bag.

"Thank you for your help, Bert. What's your plan?"

"I've got to find Dorothy Healey and talk to her."

I found a woman with a clipboard and gave her my best Biff-from-East-Hampton grin and asked if she knew where I could find Dorothy Healey. The woman was pleasant and told me to try the main dining room and pointed the way. The dining room was empty except for a couple of staff members setting silverware and glasses. Mrs. Healey was examining the flower arrangements that were in the center of each table. She wore a sleeveless yellow sundress. I walked up behind her and cleared my throat. She spun smartly and gave me a curious smile.

"Yes, may I help you?"

"Mrs. Healey, I need to talk to you, it's important."

"Are you from the florist? We're still short several centerpieces."

"No. I'm from St. Boniface. Do you remember me?" She stared at me blankly so I added quickly, "Bert Shambles. I picked up the clothing donation for the thrift shop."

"Yes, I remember." Her voice sounded far away, not nearly as vibrant as it had been just a few days earlier. And she looked as if she had aged another five years since I last saw her. "What is it you want? You're not a member here, are you?"

"No, ma'am. But I came to tell you something important." I leaned in closer. "I found it."

She looked down at my hands with that same blank expression. I don't see anything."

"I don't have it yet. Aria Tortura is on her way here now with it."

Mrs. Healey nodded like she understood, but in a way that made me think she didn't. "Oh yes, the little Tortura girl. Such lovely skin."

"She'll be here any minute. We were both worried about you, we went by your house to see if you were all right."

"Of course I was all right. Why wouldn't I be?"

"Because I thought—never mind. The point is, I found the golf club. The putter you said was missing from your husband's bag. I'm positive. I mean, I'm pretty sure it's the right one, but you'll have to confirm that."

"I have no idea what you're talking about," she said flatly. "Excuse me." She turned and walked away, through some swinging doors. Beyond the doors I could see a pantry or part of the kitchen, and several men in white hats and aprons, chopping and calling out directions in Spanish. I considered following her, but thought better of it.

I went back to where Scotty was finishing the set-up. He was checking levels, programming sounds on the keyboard, testing each new setting with a few jazzy chords.

"What's wrong? You look like you've seen a ghost."

"I have." I sat down in a side chair.

"Didn't go well?"

"She acted like I was crazy. She had no idea what I was talking about!" I dropped my head into my hands. "I'm so screwed."

"Well, not to make excuses for the lady, but I think she's under a lot of strain these days."

"She's probably worried that we figured out she's having an affair with Bill Shanley."

Scotty stopped doing his scales. "Honey, everybody has known about that for the last five, six years. If she's worried about people finding out, she's barking up the wrong tree."

"So she's really banging Shanley?"

"Such a wonderful way with words you have, Bert. But yes, she has been 'banging' him, as you so delicately put it." Scotty sighed. "He must be ten years younger than she is. What's he doing with her? To make matters worse, he's rich and handsome. Just the kind of guy I'd like to find some day. But he's always been a ladies' man, very smooth. Now that old man Healey is gone I think he's finally making his move."

"What for? If he's as smooth as you say, why choose Dorothy? She's a very pretty lady, of course, but why her?"

He stopped fidgeting with the keyboard and looked at me. "If you tell anyone I told you this I'll deny it, of course, but word is that Bill is having financial problems. I guess he took a big bet on some real estate ventures at the top of the market, and when the last crash came he lost almost everything."

"Not everything. He's still got that super-expensive car."

"He does? I never noticed. The obsession with automobiles is something you breeder boys do; I've never understood it."

"Me neither, actually, I just found out about it from the valet out front."

"Is it a clue?" His eyes widened. "Are you really an undercover agent? I bet you are. That would explain so much." His voice trailed off so I asked him to explain and he perked up again. "Like, how you seem really ditzy, disorganized, unfocused, all that, but it's all just part of your disguise. I'm right, aren't I?" I looked at him and blinked. "Maybe not," he added, "but I meant it in a good way. So what do you think you'll do about Dorothy? Does that ruin your plan?"

"I don't know. There was something else about her, something in her look. She was afraid. Almost like she was covering for someone. I gave Scotty what I hoped was a hard, secret agent kind of glare. He straightened up.

"Don't look at me, I'm not involved in anything more dishonest than the honest pursuit of the next gig. Preferably with free food and drink thrown in."

"No, not you. I bet it's that rat Shanley."

"Bill."

"That's what I'm thinking. God, what a creep."

"Bill."

"Yes, that's who I'm talking about. Why do you keep repeating it? Just hearing his name gives me the creeps. I'm going to find that no-good, wife-killing SOB and tell him that he's got some explaining to do." Scotty stopped what he was doing and stared at me, open-mouthed. "I'm serious. You know he killed his wife, right? Sure he's big, but guys like him are cowards at heart. That's why they bully people."

"Shut up, Bert."

"Why? Because we're at this fabulous so-called charity event, so rich people can congratulate themselves for shaking a few crumbs off their plate for the less fortunate? Give me a break."

"It's not that," Scotty said softly. He gestured with a chin motion. "He's standing right behind you."

Um

A hand like a bear paw gripped my upper arm, nearly crushing it. It felt like a nutcracker on a banana, and I don't have to tell you who the banana was.

"Come with me."

Bill Shanley had a deep, confident voice that immediately destroyed any cute fantasies Aria had about me intimidating him or staying in control. "I want to have a word with you."

He was big, at least six-two compared to my five-ten and a half, and built like a linebacker. He pulled me into the clubhouse. A couple of old ladies nodded and said hello as he hustled me inside. He ignored them, and dragged me behind a square wooden pillar in the corner. There was no way I could break his grip so I waited until he was about to release me and then shook him off. My upper arm was throbbing and bruised. Shanley was sweaty and tense, with a fixed look in his eyes and perspiration spots blooming on his pale blue polo shirt. He was probably between two-twenty five and two-fifty, but didn't look fat. He looked youthful, again in that corny, preppy way, with sandyish blond hair and blue eyes that looked dead, like they had just given up trying to be attractive at some point and now just beamed flashes of barely controlled fury and rage, the payoff for a lifetime of chasing the wrong things. I don't know what I had expected when I met him, but because my plan was fuzzy and vague I expected him to be that way, too. But no. Bill Shanley was depressingly present, vital, and strong. When he spoke his voice resonated inside my chest like a timpani drum.

"So you're the punk that Aria Tortura is trying to protect? What the hell do you think you two are doing? Why are you blackmailing me?"

He spoke in the form of questions, but the question marks at the end of each sentence sounded more like hooks that he wanted to gouge my eyes out with. I took a step back and swallowed once before speaking.

"Nobody's blackmailing anybody. All that's going to happen is that you're going to explain to the police why Corky Healey's clothes and missing putter were in Marcus Rogers's van, and why you were spending time with him."

"Who says I was spending time with him?"

"We do. Aria and I saw you both on the beach, getting onto your boat."

"So what? Is walking down the beach with another person a crime? Is that the best you've got?"

"I can't say any more about that. But we also know about a certain little real estate venture between you and Dorothy Healey."

Shanley rolled his eyes, but I watched his face carefully and I think it got to him. He got angry, but wasn't quite as confident as before. It lasted only a second before he recovered.

"I don't know how you know about that, but I assure you that it is completely legal and above board. It's also highly confidential, which means that however you got your hands on that information was probably illegal, which means I'm going to nail you both."

Then he took a look at my name badge and shook his head in disbelief.

"Shambles? Are you related to Jim Shambles? You're his kid, aren't you? The one who got busted. Figures you'd get caught up in something like this. Thank God you're not my kid. You're just as stupid as your old man."

I looked at him blankly. Insulting my dad didn't really bother me; I had thought of plenty of worse things to call him over the years. And there wasn't anything he could say about me or my situation that I hadn't thought of a million times already myself. I covered my mouth to stifle a yawn.

"Don't try to get a rise out of me, Billy-boy. You're finished. Aria is on her way over with the golf club. We're going to make sure everyone knows what's going on, including the cops."

"Oh, really? And just what do you think is going on?"

"We know what you were looking for in the pockets of Corky's old clothes."

"I have no idea what you're talking about."

"I'm sure. We'll see if your memory improves when Aria gets here."

"The minute she does, I will have you both arrested for blackmail, trespassing, stalking, harassment, and stealing company secrets." He grinned now, enjoying himself. "Face it, you and that little wop slut you're hanging around with have nothing on me." Shanley pointed toward the exit. "You have to leave now."

"What did you just say?"

"You heard me. Get out, now."

"Not that. Before. What did you call Aria Tortura?"

Shanley paused. When his eyes looked into mine the smile dropped from his face and I could see he lost some of the red from his cheeks. He tried to keep up his bravado but it was too late. I smelled fear.

* * *

Dear Dr. Kornbluth:

I am truly sorry for what you are about to read.

> *Sincerely,*
> *Bert Shambles*

* * *

My first left went a little loose and wide, but my knee caught a good part of his junk as I snapped my right elbow around high and tight, getting him across that dumb square jaw of his. I followed that with a smart, economical jab to the solar plexus. Then I shoved him against the pillar and stepped back to survey the damage.

Nothing.

Shanley was more amused than hurt. I took a step toward him, breathing through my teeth, ready to tear him apart or be torn apart trying.

One of the clipboard ladies stuck her head around the pillar. "Good day, Mr. Shanley." She sized me up in about half a second and shot me a dirty look. I wasn't wearing anything bright pink, bright green, bright blue or bright yellow. My shoes did not have pennies in them and I did not look like I had just stepped out of Wimbledon, or wherever the big golf tournaments are held.

"Yes, we're fine." The lady moved on and Shanley put up his hands to slow my advance.

"All right, I get your point. Fine. We'll talk when your *lady friend* gets here. Maybe I can talk some sense into her."

"I heard you've tried talking something else into her."

He ignored this. "When she gets here, the two of you call me and we'll talk. There are some private conference rooms and offices upstairs we can use."

"Maybe you should think about what to say to the cops when they interview you about Marcus."

"I think the police have better things to do than investigate why a prominent local citizen was walking down the beach with another man."

"Are you prominent enough to get away with murdering him?" I tapped my chin. "Oh wait, you already *have* gotten away with murder at least once, isn't that right?"

"What are you referring to?"

The look on his face was so extreme that I immediately regretted saying it. "Nothing. Never mind."

"I know you're making a nasty crack about my wife, who is either dead or living in Brazil with a young stud, but what are you saying about Marcus?"

"Don't act so surprised. I also saw you leaving the Healey house the other night, following the van on the night Marcus was killed. The police are going to be extremely interested."

He stared off into space, then back at me. His voice was low and even, almost robotic. "I must be running now, but nice to talk with you."

"Don't go too far, asshole."

Shanley walked off like a zombie. The jig was up, the noose was tightening, the long arm of the law was going to come down and for once it wasn't going to come down on me. It was a damn good feeling.

Scotty was playing a very nice-sounding composition that I didn't recognize. He nodded as I pulled a chair over to his side and sat down, waiting to turn the page.

"How did it go with Shanley?"

"Lousy. But he's willing to talk. How long have we been here?"

Scotty checked his watch. "I picked you up at Aria's at a quarter to, now it's half past. I'm sure Aria will be here soon."

"I hope so."

He flipped to a new piece of music and I moved my page-turning fingers into position.

After a few more numbers, we took a bathroom break. I didn't really have to go, but I didn't want to be left alone; after the initial impression of wealth and dignity wore off the place gave me the creeps.

By the time we walked back to the porch from the bathroom another fifteen minutes had gone by. I kept feeling like something was wrong. We had just sat back down when two of the valets from earlier, including the one who had shown me the Mercedes, came over. I nodded to the first guy, but he wasn't smiling.

"I'm very sorry, but you two gentlemen have to leave."

Scotty stood up. "Two? But I'm part of the entertainment?"

"Sorry, but you both came together so you both have to leave together."

"I demand to speak to Bill Shanley."

"That's who gave us the instructions."

We lugged the equipment back to the car in silence. The valets were cool about it, none of us wanted any trouble. The sun was beating down, hot and heavy. We were both sweating by the time we got the car loaded, from the exertion and the anger. Scotty was still fuming.

"The nerve of that man. I'm going to give him a piece of my mind the next time I see him."

"Sorry I got you into trouble. This was all my fault."

"No, I knew what I was doing. But if I wasn't sure about him before, about his involvement in anything sinister, now I hope he fries."

In a way I was relieved to be getting kicked out; I was worried about Aria. It had been an hour since we went our separate ways and there was still no sign or word from her. I wondered if she had been stopped by the police at the rooming-house. Maybe they had taken her to the station for questioning. Scotty must have read my silence. He started the car, and the glorious air-conditioning, and folded his hands on his lap.

"What now?"

"Maybe we can wait somewhere near the entrance, and see if her car comes. Otherwise I'll have to go back to her place and get my car, then turn myself in."

"Now that this is over, can I please ask what you were trying to put over on Shanley?"

I pulled the envelope from my back pocket. "Here. This. We found some clues to what might have happened to Corky Healey, but the main people involved are a zombie golf widow, a possibly psychopathic stockbroker, and a dead pool player from Louisiana."

"Pool player? What are you talking about?"

"Marcus Rogers. He was involved in this somehow; I just couldn't find out how in time. Now he's dead and I'm in trouble."

"Louisiana?"

"That's what his plates said."

"That's interesting. Was he by any chance tall and ugly, with red hair? Drives a nasty white van?"

"Drove. But yes, that sounds like him. Did you know him?"

"No, but I spoke to him briefly after the funeral."

"What did you say?"

"I asked him if he was a friend or family of the deceased."

"What did he say?"

"He gave me a nasty look and said 'It's none of your business.' That was the last I saw of him."

Scotty fiddled with the radio, punched a button and put the news on. "I wonder if there's any news about him, or what happened."

We sat in silence, listening to the baseball scores. Yankees won, Mets lost. Weather, hot and humid. Bert Shambles, dead meat.

I tuned out the chatter from the radio. Something was working in the back of my mind, a thought I could not really define but was bugging me all the same, like a pebble in a shoe that I couldn't reach. I might not be the swiftest knife in the toolbox sometimes, but I'm not a complete idiot. My mind just works slower than some people's. Okay, most people's. But it's the brain I've got and the one I've got to work with, so I make peace with my limitations the best that I can. I closed my eyes and thought it over. I kept going back to Shanley, how nasty he was, and the insults he said to me. The stuff he said did hurt, but I had long ago learned how to control that pain, put it somewhere safe, or at least out of reach. Sometimes it was the only way I could get through the day. *Thank God you're not my son.*

"We have to go," I said to Scotty. "Start driving."

"What about Aria? I thought we were waiting for her."

"No time. I need you to do me another solid."

Scotty put the car into drive and we rolled off the shoulder onto the road. "Where to, master?"

"The Healey house."

Scotty sighed heavily. "You're just a sucker for punishment, aren't you?"

Well now

A few minutes later we were in front of the house. I thanked Scotty and got out.

"Do you want me to wait here for you?"

"No. I don't want you getting into any more trouble on my account. I'll get myself home."

"At least you're a cheap date," he said, then blew me a kiss and rolled away.

I rang the bell, waited, rang again, waited, knocked and waited. Nothing. Then I went down to the garage and punched in the code and the door opened. My palms were sweaty and my heart was racing, but this time I knew exactly where I was going and what I was looking for. I went through the lower level and game room and up the stairs to the living room. The silver picture frame was still on the side table, where Aria had left it. I picked it up and looked at the picture, feeling a momentary pang of regret for the experiences I never had. The happy family on the beach, tanned, healthy and wealthy and looking like they didn't have a care in the world. But you did have a care, Corky, didn't you?

I heard the sound of a guitar playing, a familiar melody. It sounded like the music from "Wonderful Tonight." I looked around and realized the sound was coming from my pants. I pulled out Aria's phone.

"Hello?"

"Meet me at the sixth hole right now if you know what's good for you." It was Bill Shanley.

"I'm not quite that dumb," I said. "Any talking we need to do we're going to do in a more public place."

"You'll be here if you ever want to see your girlfriend again," he said. "If you tell anyone, or call the police, she dies."

The line went dead.

I ran downstairs and went out through the sliding doors, across the gently sloping acres, past Corky Healy's putting green—now overgrown and untended—and through the hedges onto the golf course of the Pondington Country Club. The only time I had been there was at night, so it looked completely unfamiliar in the daylight. I followed the flags, hoping they were in some kind of numerical order. I went the wrong direction at first but got the hang of it.

It was hot. The polyester-blend work pants I had bought at Sears weren't cutting it. Sweat poured out of me. With all the running I was doing I thought I should at least invest in some good track shoes and maybe one of those cool jogging suits with the stripes going down the sides. Or maybe a pair of cleats to stomp on Bill Shanley's ugly face. No. I was cool, cooler than cool. I was in love. I was crazy. I couldn't lose.

I wouldn't lose.

Running backwards from hole seven I caught sight of the split fairway that Dale had told me about, with the wooded area in the middle. From a distance it was too shaded for me to see anybody, so I slowed down as I walked across the grass. I was completely in the open, a sitting duck. My heart pounded with fear but also rage that Bill Shanley would try to hurt the woman I loved. I would die protecting her if I had to. I hoped I didn't have to.

When I was about twenty yards away, they came out of the woods. Shanley had a golf club—*the* golf club—across Aria's neck, forcing her to arch her back while walking forward. Aria's mouth was bound with some kind of scarf. She looked so tiny and helpless compared to his hulking, dumb, linebacker frame that it took all my effort not to charge him. I took a few quick steps as a natural reaction, but Bill pulled the putter tighter and Aria gasped.

"That's close enough. Now give me what you found and it will all be over."

"Let her go, Bill. You know this is crazy. You can't seriously think you're going to get away with this."

"Give me the information or she dies. It's self-defense. You don't know who you're messing with. Where is it?"

I reached into my back pocket and removed the decoy envelope, with one of the brochures from the resort inside. I took a few steps closer, slowly, then placed the envelope on the ground and stepped back.

"Okay, now let her go and we'll just walk away. It's over."

"No. Not until I have proof. Open it up and show it to me."

I was close enough now to get a good look at him. He was in a bad way. Sweat darkened his polo shirt and dripped from his chin. His voice was an imitation of his earlier anger, still full of rage but also trembling, like he had lost his mind. I picked up the envelope. I started to reach in, thought better of it, and then grinned at Shanley.

"You really want this?"

"You know I do. Shut up and show me or I'll hurt her."

I looked at Aria. Tears were streaming down her face. She grunted, breathing heavily, too weak to fight. I held the envelope out with both hands.

And started tearing it down the middle.

"What the hell are you doing?"

"I've changed my mind, Billy-boy. I think anybody who roughs up a young woman isn't a man, and doesn't deserve to win. You have to make a choice right now, let her go or I destroy this."

My fingers moved again. Shanley gargled with an animal fury and pulled on the putter. Aria cried a muffled scream through the scarf and her feet lifted off the ground. She looked nearly unconscious.

Maybe it wasn't such a good idea after all.

"Stop it!"

Another figure came out of the trees and underbrush. It was Dorothy Healey. She was holding what I was pretty sure was a shotgun. She looked like she could handle it very well. She turned the gun on Shanley.

"The young man is right, Bill. Let her go."

Bill wavered. He looked at me, and Dorothy, and his grip slackened slightly. At that moment Aria's eyes opened wide, and in one expert motion she slammed her foot down on his and rammed her elbow into his gut, hard. Shanley wheezed and doubled over. Aria was free. She staggered away from him and fell to her knees, gasping and rubbing her neck.

"Thank God you're here," I said to Mrs. Healey. "I think I figured out what's been going on."

"Oh, did you?" Dorothy came over to me, sidestepping, the gun still trained on Bill. She balanced the gun expertly in her right hand and held out her left. "Give it to me."

"Mrs. Healey, there's something I have to tell you—"

"Now."

I complied. She pulled out the brochure and laughed.

"You stupid idiot." She spat the words at Bill. "I told you they were bluffing, and like an idiot you fell for it. That's why your business is failing and your life is a mess."

Shanley looked at Dorothy helplessly, his eyes empty. Then he looked at Aria and his face snapped with renewed fury. He raised the club. Aria screamed and tried shielding herself.

It's true what they say about life-or-death situations. Things really do slow down, and just a few seconds can seem like hours. I remember seeing something on PBS one night about how the faster things move, like light, the more time slows down. I'm pretty sure that's what they said.

Anyway, I think adrenaline must have the same effect, because it seemed like I had all the time in the world to go over to Aria, push her out of the way, and get my arm up to take the blow. The club connected with the soft part of my forearm. The pain was blinding, evil and insane. I actually saw stars.

I fell to my knees, clutching my left arm. Bill dropped the putter and held his arms out to Mrs. Healey.

"Please, Dotty, don't let it end like this. I love you."

The blast from the gun is a sound I will never forget. Needles of fire peppered my shoulder. My ears rang from the sound and everything got wobbly. I soon felt the warm, ticklish sensation of liquid running down my back. Aria screamed my name and wrapped her arms around me, cradling me. When I looked up, I saw Bill looking down dumbly at his shirt, as a red constellation of ruin spread across his chest. He looked dead before he hit the ground.

My head was heavy and the world around me was blinking on and off as I lost consciousness, like the lights in a theater lobby at the end of intermission. I turned and saw Mrs. Healey, gun still aimed, only now it was pointed at Aria and me. Behind her I saw what I assumed was a mirage, brought on by my injuries. In the distance, something that looked like a golf cart was heading our way. The strange thing was that the person who was driving the cart looked like he was in a purple robe, covered in moons and stars. His beard and wild hair were flying, but in slow motion. Someone who looked very much like Daddy-O was in the passenger seat, and a person who looked like Scotty was in the back.

Dorothy Healey had no time to react; by the time she heard it, there was no chance to get out of the way. It slammed into her legs and sent her and the gun flying. She wailed from the impact and crumpled to a heap on the ground. Then there was a slow rippling across the atmosphere, and a deep humming like giant engines or machinery somewhere, then the ground opened up to swallow me and everything went black.

After

I was in the hospital for two nights. My arm wasn't too bad, just a hairline fracture in my forearm and a few stitches to my upper left back and shoulder where some stray buckshot hit me. I caught a good portion of the blow from Shanley on my head, and because of the earlier hit I took from Marcus at the Slosh, the doctors wanted to keep me to make sure I didn't have any brain damage. They didn't find any, which only proves that doctors don't know everything.

They also gave me some great drugs, which took the pain away but also made me lose my inhibitions. I talked to the police several times, and told them everything— sneaking into the Healey house twice, breaking into the van, swinging the club at Marcus. The cops got such a kick out of the story that I wondered if I had to keep repeating it just so they could hear it again for their own entertainment. But that might have been the drugs, I don't know. I knew that I might be screwing myself royally by admitting every illegal thing I had done, but I just didn't care anymore. I talked and talked and flirted with the nurses, ate the crummy food and dozed in and out of consciousness. It was a pretty good vacation overall.

My mom brought me food from the deli and any newspapers that had any stories about what happened. I was mentioned in a few of them, which I clipped and saved for my scrapbook, if I ever have one someday. Mom was upset and freaked out but also said she was proud of me, which meant a lot. For once I was involved with the police in a positive way. It was progress.

I gathered from the newspapers and sporadic TV accounts that Bill Shanley was pronounced dead at the scene, like I thought. Mrs. Healey was in custody and undergoing psychiatric evaluations, and facing a wide range of charges. There was alternating speculation about either a self-defense strategy or insanity plea.

I was just waking up from a nice drug-induced nap when I saw Daddy-O sitting next to the bed, fiddling with his phone. He heard me stir and looked up from what he was doing.

"How are you doing, slugger?"

"I've been better. How did you wind up on the golf course?"

"That lady friend of yours, Aria, called me. She's really something else, that gal. I tried calling you back after that message you left me, especially after I followed up and found that there really was a dead guy with a white van with Louisiana plates. She called me back from your phone, said you were in trouble and to meet her at the country club. I got there as quick as I could. Dorothy Healey had already intercepted Aria by the time I got there, and got her out to that quiet spot on the golf course, where she had a gun. She thought you were in league with Bill, and that you were going to try pinning the murder of her husband on her with the putter."

"Pin a murder? I just wanted a damn five hundred dollar reward. She must be crazy."

Daddy-O looked at his notebook. "You know, for a guy on probation, who's allegedly not crazy, and who allegedly knows that he is *supposed* to be on his best behavior at all times, you certainly racked up a lot of offenses. Let's see now...breaking and entering, trespassing, menacing."

"All right, I get it. You're saying I'm screwed, right?"

He closed the notebook. "No, you're in the clear. I heard some of the detectives out in the hallway. They're calling you a hero. What you did took real guts. You'll be free to go when the doctor releases you."

I felt a buzz rush through my body, one that definitely was not caused by the drugs. It was relief.

"Did I see my neighbor Aku driving a golf cart?"

"Yes. He came with Aria, for support. I guess they got separated, and Aku wound up doing tarot card readings for the fundraiser, before everything went crazy. That musician, Scotty, was making a big stink at the gates of the country club when I pulled up, so he filled me in with what he could. You've got a lot of cool friends, Bert."

"I guess I do."

"Oh, and your hunch was right. The Rogers woman has confirmed it, for the record. She and Corky Healey did have an affair approximately 25 years ago, and it did produce a child, and that child was—"

"Marcus."

He nodded. "She never told anyone who the father was. Corky didn't know until a few months ago. I guess Dorothy found out about the affair around the same time Ms. Rogers learned she was pregnant, and Corky broke off the relationship before she had a chance to tell him. According to Ms. Rogers, Judy, she didn't want to burden him with having to make a choice, and possibly hurting Dorothy or Dale in the process."

"So if Marcus didn't know who his father was, how did he get involved at all?"

"Corky was dead set against using his name or likeness for any commercial purposes; that never changed. But Dorothy and Bill kept planning anyway, for when he died. They started their affair about five years ago and started planning the deal from the beginning. It's not clear who initiated the affair, but they were both on board with it. Bill's financial problems were mounting and he needed a big deal to keep him in business. So he started digging for any dirt he could find. At some point Dorothy mentioned the affair, and the name of the woman, and Shanley took it from there. Private detective, the works. Based on Marcus Rogers's age and physical features it wasn't hard to figure out the truth. He had the detective pose as an attorney, saying that Corky Healey was old and frail and wanted to make amends and take care of his former lover and meet his son."

"A bluff."

"Right. But it worked. Ms. Rogers wanted to do the right thing, and make sure Marcus had a chance to meet his dad if he wanted, so she confirmed that Corky was the father and Bill had his leverage. He blackmailed Corky, basically. Corky agreed to sign over all rights to his likeness and name for the resort to Bill, on condition that he first meet Marcus in person. Which turned out to be trickier than he thought, because at this point Dorothy still didn't know about Marcus, and because she kept an eagle eye on her husband and managed all his affairs, right down to the minute."

"She must have loved him very much," I said. Daddy-O shook his head.

"Or despised him. From what I can gather the marriage was never a success, which is what led Corky to looking for other opportunities when he was married to a beautiful woman like Dorothy, who was still young when the affair happened. Maybe thirty, thirty-five tops."

"Okay, so they had to arrange a meeting, something that wouldn't arouse too much suspicion."

"Right. That's why the golf course, early in the morning. It was Corky's routine still, every morning, and the one place where Dorothy wouldn't follow him or keep him under her thumb."

"Sounds like a good plan. So what happened?"

"It was a classic double-cross. Shanley was trying to gain Marcus Rogers' trust, by offering him a piece of the new business. He set Marcus up in an apartment in Queens, in a building he owns, to give the two of them time to meet. We're learning most of this from Dorothy, of course, so we have to take it with a grain of salt."

"How did she find out about it?"

"From what I've been able to gather, it seems that when the legal papers were being drawn up, someone from the attorney's office accidentally left a message on Dorothy Healey's phone by mistake. She had spent the night at Shanley's house, and heard the message on her way home. She felt like her husband and boyfriend were conspiring against her, and I guess she snapped. So when she got home early that morning she went out to the golf course to confront him there."

"Knowing that if Marcus was on his way, then she could kill Corky and pin it on him?"

Daddy-O levered his hand side to side. "Mmm, maybe. We're not sure Dorothy intended to kill Corky that morning. She may have been more interested in confronting Corky and Marcus at the same time, but things got a bit out of hand. Or maybe it really was an accident. Dorothy's not making much sense on that point yet."

"But there's no chance she's going to be released any time soon?"

"No way. She's in big trouble no matter what."

"Good. Because I saw how she handles a gun."

"Look, Bert, there's something else I need to tell you, and you're not going to like it."

I blinked my eyes at him, full of innocence.

"What could possibly upset me? It's not like you're sleeping with my ex-girlfriend or anything." Daddy-O winced visibly when I said this, looked down at the floor and rubbed his forehead.

"Ah. So you know. I'm truly sorry about that. I never planned it, never meant for anything to happen. I interviewed her as a routine part of my background research on you and your case. One thing led to another."

"It's okay, just be careful around her."

"Yeah, I'm starting to figure that out. How did you know we were dating?"

"I saw the two of you in Brooklyn, outside your office."

"You did? When?"

"When I tried returning this."

I reached over to the side table with my good arm. Underneath the pile of newspapers was the gold Cross pen.

"So that's where it was. I thought it was lost."

Daddy-O started to take it, stopped. "Would you like to keep it?"

"Booby prize? You get the girl, I get a used pen?"

"No. I was thinking more like, maybe we could be less like cop and criminal and more like friends."

"Sure." I put the pen back on the table. "Just don't expect any goddamned relationship advice from me."

There was a knock on the door. Daddy-O got up and answered, turned to me and smiled.

"You have a far more important visitor here. I'll catch you later, Bert."

"Thanks for the pen, Officer D'Addario."

He grinned. "Hey, call me Daddy-O."

"I already do." He shook his head and was gone.

She came in. She had on white tennis shorts, a pink Izod shirt, and Stan Smiths. I wanted to scoop her up and put her in a waffle cone. She also looked helpless, hands clasped, eyes wide and shiny with pre-tears. She didn't say a word, but ran over to the bed and threw her arms over me, and started kissing my face.

"You are the bravest, most wonderful man I have ever met," she whispered. "I've been so worried about you."

"How are you doing?"

"I'm okay, just a sore throat from where that creep choked me. No damage. I'm also still in a bit of shock, but that's already wearing off."

"How are things at home?"

"I told my folks everything. They actually listened to me for once, and they're going to handle it. They're going to say that the money was found stashed somewhere and that everything is fine."

"What about me? I was still caught with the bag."

"No, that's totally fine. You're in the clear. I explained that I put it there, and that you were really another victim. Everyone is so happy that the money is back. Nobody from my family is going to hurt you. In fact, my father wants you to call him when you're feeling better, so he can thank you personally."

It was a nice thought, but as far as that phone call was concerned I would not be feeling better for a long time. I grinned, thinking about this.

"Are you all right? You look pretty zonked out."

"I'm fine. I'm just on drugs."

"Oh." Aria smoothed the sheet of the bed with her hand. She had a worried expression now.

"What's wrong?"

"I'm moving out of my parents' house. I'll be living with my cousins Joanna and Regina for a while."

My mind reeled, thinking of the fun Aria and I would have as soon as she got her own place. I bet she'd have cable.

I propped myself up. "That's fantastic. I'll be over to cook for you every night. Provided you like microwave burritos, of course." She shook her head. "Oh, that's right. No canned tomatoes. I'll figure out something to cook for you."

"Bert, wait. You don't understand. My cousins live in San Diego."

Just like that, my whole world went dark again.

"Are your parents sending you away? Is this because of me?"

"No. This is something I need. I've been needing this ever since high school, something that goes way beyond you and me. That's what makes it so sad. I finally meet a boy I'd love to get to know better, and I get my first chance to really live on my own. If we become involved now, then I'll be stuck on Long Island and never get off."

"I understand completely," I said. "I'm heartbroken, but I understand. How long will you be there?"

"I don't know. A few months, maybe more. I won't know for sure until I actually experience that freedom and have time to think about things. But I'll miss you like crazy. I hope you'll be able to come visit."

"I'd love to."

Aria perked up at this. She held up a small gift bag.

"What's this?"

"Nothing much. Just a little gift for, oh, I don't know, like saving my life or something."

We both giggled like kids and I removed the box. It was wrapped in very nice, heavy paper. It was a cellphone.

"It's not fancy, but you can surf the web and get cool games and apps for it and stuff. Do you like it?"

"It's amazing, thank you."

"I got it as an extra line on my plan, so you don't have to pay anything to use it. I won't hear any arguments about that. And you can set up your own passwords and stuff, so you don't have to worry about me prying into your busy social life."

"What social life?"

"Now that you're a hero, you're going to have girls throwing themselves at you."

"They can throw themselves, but there's only girl I want to catch. Can I see you before you go?"

"I doubt it. I leave in a couple of days. I'll be pretty swamped between now and then. I'm sorry this is so sudden, but it's not entirely up to me. I still did a really bad thing in the eyes of my parents, and they're not going to trust me for quite some time."

"I understand."

"Speaking of them, I better be going."

Aria gave me another one of her best-in-class kisses. She stroked her fingertips along my face and in combination with the narcotics my whole body buzzed with contentment. Then she was gone.

I turned on the phone and played with it. A minute later it made a noise and a window popped up, telling me I had a message from Aria. I figured out how to open it. It was the recipe for the pasta dish she had made for me at the rooming-house.

God, how I loved that woman.

And so

Fr. Pete cut his vacation short. He came by the hospital, said a prayer for me and did some healing mumbo-jumbo, after promising me that it wasn't Last Rites. He told me to take as much time off as I needed, and that he would keep me on with full pay until I was ready to return. He's nice like that. He also said that St. Boniface was in full crisis mode, with two of its most prominent families involved in a shocking scandal, so it would probably be better if I kept a low profile until the hoopla died down. I told him I had no problem with that.

Scotty sent flowers, with a card that said that because of the notoriety of the case he was booked solid with gigs through the end of the year. It ended with, "Getting kicked out of that fundraiser was the best thing that's ever happened to me!" That made one of us.

There were some benefits for me as well. I became something of a local celebrity down at the Slosh; Ruby and Oscar greeted me like a returning war hero, and I had lots of strangers coming up to me and shaking my hand. Cute girls weren't exactly throwing themselves at me, but maybe I didn't hang out in enough places where cute girls might be. The only cute girl I wanted was in San Diego, anyway.

A couple of weeks later I was still buzzing, a combination of the lingering excitement plus the prescription painkillers I had gotten when I left the hospital. I was lying on the cot one night, watching a show about zebras and drinking my way through a six-pack, when the home phone rang.

"Is this Bert Shambles?"

"Yes?"

"Dale Healey. Is this a convenient time?"

I propped myself up in bed. "It's fine. What's up?"

"You're not going to believe this. Do you have a minute to talk?"

The following afternoon I was rolling down the leafy streets of Pondington, on my way once again to the Healey house. I rang the bell and a moment later Dale opened the door and I went in. He looked tired and lost. We shook hands.

"Thanks for coming over."

"Glad to. I want to say again how very sorry I am for what has happened."

He shook his head as he stared into space. "I still can't believe it. It's all a bad dream. To lose my father and mother within a few weeks, plus a brother I never knew I had." His voice trailed off and he ran his fingers through his hair. "Then this happened. It's like a never-ending nightmare."

"Where are they?"

I followed Dale through the house, to the staircase down to the game room. There was a mound of black plastic garbage bags piled next to the pool table.

"Someone from the property unit contacted me after the van was removed from impound. After all the bad things that have happened, we still can't get rid of these clothes. It's like a horror movie."

"I give you my word that you will not see them again."

"I hope not. Are you bringing them back to St. Boniface?"

"No. The store is actually closed for the summer. But I know a place in Brooklyn that will take them. They actually pay for good stuff, so if you want me to let you know—" Dale waved me off.

"No need. In fact, I owe you money. My mom promised a reward to whoever found the putter, and you kept your end of the bargain. Do you want me to write you a check?"

I shook my head. "No, but thank you for offering. Your mom wasn't thinking very clearly. I really hope she comes through this all right."

"She tried to kill you."

"Nobody's perfect."

I pulled the Olds down to the garage. Dale was waiting with two bags. We loaded them into the trunk and went back in. I only had my right hand to use; Dale saw me struggling with a bag and told me to take it easy and he would do the work. I said that would be fine, but only because I wasn't carrying any laundry in the car. Dale kicked one of the bags.

"The only mystery of this whole thing is what Bill and Marcus were looking for. I've searched everything two, three times. I've turned the house upside down."

"Nothing?"

"Nothing but loose change and old scorecards."

"Are you sure you've checked everywhere? Coats, jackets, briefcases, anything like that?"

"Again and again."

Dale brought another couple of bags out to the car and returned. "I've changed the code to the garage door, by the way. Just in case you were thinking of moving in."

"Sorry about that."

"Considering the circumstances, knowing that you broke into my house a couple of times seems minor by comparison."

I rolled a striped pool ball down the length of the table, remembering the brief time Aria and I had spent there. "The first time I was here, picking up the clothes, you told me that your dad was taking lessons."

"No, he wasn't taking lessons yet, but he was going to start."

"Who was his instructor going to be?"

Dale shrugged. "No clue. I think my mom must have found someone. No, wait. Bill set it up, I remember now."

"But you don't know who he was using as a teacher."

"No. Nothing. I just know that the guy was going to be coming in from the city. Why?"

"Did you know that Marcus was a pool player?"

"I didn't." His eyes narrowed onto mine. "Do you think?"

"No idea. Just saying."

Dale looked at the table. "That sly old dog. My dad was probably going to hire Marcus to teach him, so they could spend some time together as father and son and my mom and I would never have been any wiser."

"There was a bit of a family resemblance."

"Twenty, thirty years ago, yes. But my dad was quite old and didn't look the same anymore."

"And if they were going to be playing pool, and spending time together..."

"What?"

"Hold on a sec."

I went around the table. It was one of those fancy models, with the woven leather pockets.

Pockets.

I reached into each hole and pulled out the balls, then fished around. Dale realized what I was doing and took the other side of the table. The first few we tried revealed nothing, then I reached the far corner pocket. I removed the balls and fished around. There was an indentation in the wood against the back of the pocket. I pushed and a button or switch of some kind went in, and a hidden tray popped out a few inches from the side of the table just underneath. I pulled it out with one hand and Dale took it and placed it on the red felt surface of the table. It was a low, flat wooden box, about the size of a sheet of typing paper but about two inches deep. Dale looked at the box for a moment, then at me.

"Would you like me to leave?"

"Yes. No, actually. It might be good to have a witness."

"Just don't ask me to lie for you. Unless you have a gun, in which case I'd be glad to."

He spun the box around until he found the catch. He opened it slowly. I stepped back anyway, in case it was personal. After a couple of minutes he turned and looked at me.

"It's nothing," he said. "I can't believe it. Nothing."

Dale held up one hand. There was a glossy photograph, about eight by ten. It was another picture of Corky, but this time he was with a lovely red-haired woman with a huge grin. She was cute—not beautiful in a Ruby or Aria way, but radiant and happy. That was the first thing I noticed, how happy they both looked. Corky didn't have that same strained, constipated smile. There was a free, wild kind of joy in his rugged features, and the way they looked together put a lump in my throat. Natural, perfect, and in love. I wanted to tell Dale that it wasn't nothing, that in fact that picture really was worth a thousand words, maybe a million—about a lifetime together that never happened, for two people who met each other when it was too late for either of them to do anything about it. One thing I knew was that Corky had seen this woman more than once, and their affair was hardly a one-night stand. They were in love, soul mates, or else the words have no meaning. It was an insight I decided to keep to myself.

"There's a letter too. My dad wrote it by hand, to Marcus. He said that this was the only copy of the only picture of him and Judy—I guess that's his mother's name—together, and that he had cherished this photo for all these years. He apologizes for not knowing about him sooner, and promises to make things as right as he can." Dale turned it over, then back. "That's it."

"No check? No money? No promises about addendums to any wills or anything?"

"Nope. Nothing. At the end of the letter he says, 'I will love you as my son the best I can, with the time that I have left.' That's it."

"Sounds like your dad had his heart in the right place," I said. "Other guys might have tried buying their way out. Your dad wanted to give your brother love, and a feeling of being wanted. He wanted to spend time with him. That's worth a lot more than money."

Dale considered this, nodding. When he looked up again I could see the tears. "Thank you, Bert. I think I'd better be alone right now. I have to get used to it." I made a move as if to hug him, or at least shake his hand, but Dale had gone somewhere deep inside. I nodded, picked up the last bag, and carried it out to the Olds with my good arm.

THE END

ABOUT THE AUTHOR

 Tim Hall was a journalist, musician, bike messenger and moving man before turning to the lucrative world of independent publishing. *Dead Stock* is his first mystery novel. He lives in New York City. His personal website can be fund at www.timhallbooks.com.